The Stone Axe of Burkamukk

The Stone Axe of Burkamukk

Mary Grant Bruce

MINT EDITIONS

The Stone Axe of Burkamukk was first published in 1922.

This edition published by Mint Editions 2021.

ISBN 9781513295916 | E-ISBN 9781513297415

Published by Mint Editions®

MINT
EDITIONS

minteditionbooks.com

Publishing Director: Jennifer Newens
Design & Production: Rachel Lopez Metzger
Project Manager: Micaela Clark
Typesetting: Westchester Publishing Services

CONTENTS

Foreword

Year by year the old black tribes are dying out, and many of their legends and beliefs are dying with them. These legends deal with the world as the blacks knew it; with the Bush animals and birds; the powers of storm, flood, fire, thunder, and magic, and the beings who they thought controlled these powers; with the sun, moon and stars; and with the life and death of men and women.

Many of the old tales are savage enough, but through them runs a thread of feeling for the nobler side of life, so far as these wild people could grasp it. The spirit of self-sacrifice is seen in them, and greed, selfishness and cruelty are often punished as they deserve. We are apt to look on the blacks as utter barbarians, but, as we read their own old stories, we see that they were boys and girls, men and women, not so unlike us in many ways, and that they could admire what we admire in each other, and condemn what we would condemn. The folk-tales of a people are the story of its soul, and it would be a pity if the native races of our country were to vanish altogether before we had collected enough of their legends to let their successors know what manner of people lived in Australia for thousands of years before the white man came. Some valuable collections have indeed been made, but they are all too few; and there must even today be many people, especially in the wilder parts of Australia, who are in touch with the aborigines, and could, if they would, get the old men and women to tell them the stories which were handed down to them when they were children.

In the hope of persuading all young Australians who have the opportunity to collect and preserve what they can of the ancient life and legends of Australia, I have put into modern English a few of the tales which may still be had from some old blackfellow or gin.

M.G.B.

I

The Stone Axe of Burkamukk

Chapter I

The camp lay calm and peaceful under the spring sunlight. Burkamukk, the chief, had chosen its place well: the wurleys were built in a green glade well shaded with blackwood and boobyalla trees, and with a soft thick carpet of grass, on which the black babies loved to roll. Not a hundred yards away flowed a wide creek; a creek so excellent that it fed a swamp a little farther on. The blacks loved to be near a swamp, for it was as good as a storehouse of food: the women used to go there for lily-pads and sedge-roots, and the men would spear eels in its muddy waters, while at times big flocks of duck settled on it, besides other water-fowl. Burkamukk was a very wise chief, and all his people were fat, and therefore contented.

As blacks count wealth, the people of Burkamukk were very well off. They had plenty of skin rugs, so that no one went cold, even in the winter nights; and the women had made them well, sewing them together with the sinews of animals, using for their needles the small bone of a kangaroo's hind-leg, ground to a fine point. It was hard work to sew these well, but the men used to take pains to get good skins, pegging them out with tea-tree spikes and dressing them with wood-ashes and fat, which they rubbed in until the skins were soft and supple; and so the women thought that the least they could do was to sew them in the very best way. Being particular about the rugs made the women particular about other things as well, and they had a far better outfit than could be found in most camps. Each woman had a good pitchi, a small wooden trough hollowed out of the soft wood of the bean-tree, in which food was kept. When the tribe went travelling the pitchi was as useful as a suit-case is to a white Australian girl; the lubras packed them with food, and carried them balanced on their heads, or slung to one hip by a plait of human hair, or a fur band; and sometimes a big pitchi was made by a proud father and beautifully carved with a stone knife, and used as a cradle for a fat black baby. Then the women used to weave baskets made of a strong kind of rush, ornamented with coloured patterns and fancy stitches, and each one had, as well, a bag made of the tough inner bark of the acacia tree, or sometimes of a messmate or stringy bark, in which she kept food, sticks and tinder for starting a fire, wattle-gum for cement, shells, tools, and all sorts of charms to keep off evil spirits. They had a queer kind of cooking-pot, in which they used to dissolve gum and manna. These pots were made out of the big rough lumps that grow out of old gum-trees, hollowed out by a chisel made of a kangaroo's thighbone. The women used to put gum and manna in these and place them near the fire, so that the water gradually heated without burning the wood. There was no pottery among the blacks, and so they could never boil food, but they contrived to make pleasant warm drinks in these wooden pots.

When it came to baking, however, the women of the tribe were well able to turn out toothsome roasts. Their ovens were holes in the ground, plastered with mud, and then filled with fire until the clay was very hot. When the temperature was right the embers were taken out, and the holes lined with wet grass. The food—flesh, fish, or roots—was packed in rough rush baskets and placed in the ovens, and covered with more wet grass, hot stones, gravel, and earth, until the holes were quite air-tight. The women liked to do this in the evening, so that the food cooked slowly all night; and often all the cooking was done in a few big ovens, and next morning each family came to remove its basket of food. And if you had come along breakfastless just as the steaming baskets were taken out, and had been asked to join in eating a plump young bandicoot or wallaby or a fat black fish—well, even though there were no plates or knives or forks, I do not think you would have grumbled at your meal.

The men of Burkamukk's tribe were well armed. Their boomerangs, spears and throwing-sticks were all of the best, and they had, in addition, knives made of splinters of flint or sharpened mussel-shell, lashed into handles. Some had skinning knives made of the long front teeth of the bandicoot, with the jaw left on for a handle; and they worked kangaroo bones into all kinds of tools. But Burkamukk himself had a wonderful weapon, the only one in all that district—a mighty axe. It was made of green stone, wedge-shaped, and sharply ground at one edge. This was grasped in the bend of a doubled piece of split sapling, and tightly bound round with kangaroo sinews; and the handle thus formed was additionally strengthened by being cemented to the head by a mixture of gum and shell lime. It was not a very easy matter to make that cement. First, mussel shells were burned to make the lime, and pounded in a hollow stone. Then wattle-gum was chewed for a long time and placed between sheets of green bark, which were laid in a shallow hole in the ground and covered with hot ashes until the gum was dissolved, when it was kneaded with the lime into a tough paste. The blacks would have been badly off without that cement, but not all of them would go to the trouble of making it as thoroughly as did the men of Burkamukk's tribe. All the best workmanship had gone to the manufacture of Burkamukk's axe, and the whole tribe was proud of it. Sometimes the chief would lend it to the best climbers among his young men, who used it to cut steps in the bark of trees when they wanted to climb in search of monkey-bears or 'possums; or he would let them use it to strip sheets of bark from the trees, to make their wurleys. Those to whom the axe was lent always showed their sense of the honour done them by making payment in kind—the fattest of the game caught, or a finely-woven rush mat, would be laid at the chief's door. If this had not been done Burkamukk would probably have looked wise next time some one had wished to borrow his axe, and would have remarked that he had work for it himself.

Even though he occasionally lent the axe, Burkamukk never let it go out of his sight. It was far too precious a possession for that. He, too, went hunting when the axe went, or watched it used to prise great strips of thick bark off the trees, and he probably worried the borrower very much by continually directing how it should be handled. Not that the young men would have taken any risks with it. It was the chief's axe, but its possession brought dignity upon the whole tribe. Other chiefs had axes, more or less excellent, but there was no weapon in all the countryside so famous as the axe of Burkamukk. I doubt whether the Kings of England have valued their Crown Jewels so highly as Burkamukk valued his stone treasure with the sapling handle. Certainly they cannot have found them half so useful.

On this spring afternoon Burkamukk was coming up from the swamp where he had been spearing eels. He had been very successful: Koronn, his wife, walked behind him carrying a dozen fine specimens, and thinking how good a supper she would be able to cook, and how delighted her little boy Tumbo would be; for of all things Tumbo loved to eat eel. Just at the edge of the camp Burkamukk stopped, frowning.

A hunting-party of young men had evidently just returned; they were the centre of a group in the middle of the camp, and still they were carrying their spears and throwing-sticks. They were talking loudly and gesticulating, and it was clear that those who listened to them were excited and distressed; there were anxious faces and the women were crying "Yakai!" (Alas!). The chief strode up to the group.

"What is the matter?" he asked.

The men turned, saluting him respectfully.

"We have fallen upon evil times, Chief," their leader answered. "Little game have we caught, and we have lost Kon-garn."

"Lost him! How?"

"There is a great and terrible beast in the country to which we went," answered Tullum, the young warrior. "The men of the friendly tribe we passed told us of him, but we thought they were joking with us, for it seemed a foolish tale, only fit to make women afraid. They told us of a great kangaroo they call Kuperee, larger than a dozen kangaroos and fiercer than any animal that walks on the earth; and they warned us not to go near his country."

"A kangaroo as large as a dozen!" said Burkamukk. "Ky! but I would like to see such a beast The whole tribe could feed on him."

"Ay, they might, if one had the luck to be able to kill him," said Tullum sorrowfully. "But a kangaroo of that size is no joke to encounter."

"What!" said Burkamukk. "Do you mean me to believe that there is truly such a kangaroo?"

"There is indeed," Tullum answered. "We also did not believe. We went on, thinking that the other tribe merely wished to keep us away from a good hunting-ground. We took no precautions, and we came upon him suddenly."

"And he was a big kangaroo, do you say?"

Tullum flung out his hands.

"There are no words to tell you of his bigness, O, Chief!" he said—and his voice shook with terror. "Never has such an animal been seen before. Black is he, and huge, and fierce; and when he saw us he roared and rushed upon us. There was no time to do battle: he was on us almost before one could fling a spear. Kon-garn was nearest, and he went down with one blow of the monster's foot, his head crushed. Me he struck at, but luckily for me I was almost out of his reach. Still, he touched me—see!" He moved aside his 'possum-skins, and showed long wounds, running from his shoulder to his wrist—wounds that looked as though they had been made by great claws.

Burkamukk looked at them closely.

"No small beast did that," he said. "You are lucky to be alive, Tullum."

"Ay," said Tullum briefly. "Indeed, I thought for a while that I was as dead as Kon-garn. But I managed to dodge behind a tree, and the bush was thick, so that by great good fortune I got away. Kuperee gave chase, but we all scattered, and luckily the one he chose to follow was Woma, who is the swiftest of us all; and Woma gave him the slip without much trouble, for Kuperee is so great that he cannot get through the trees quickly. So we came together again after a day and a night, and travelled home swiftly."

"And none of you went back to avenge Kon-garn?" the chief asked, sternly.

Tullum looked at him with a curious mixture of shame and defiance.

"Nay," he said. "None of us have ever been reckoned cowards—and yet we did not go back. An ordinary enemy would not have made us afraid, but there is something about Kuperee that turns the very heart to water. We hated ourselves—we hate ourselves still—for not going back. The blood of Kon-garn cries out to us for vengeance on his slayer, and in our sleep we see our comrade, with his head crushed by that terrible foot. And yet we could not turn. We have come home to you like frightened children, and shame is on our heads. We know not how to face Kon-garn's wife, who sits there and cries 'Yakai!' before her wurley."

Another of the warriors, Woma the Swift-footed, spoke up, with sullen anger in his voice.

"We are shamed," he said, "but there is Magic in it. No true animal is Kuperee, but an evil spirit. No man could possibly stand before him."

To put anything they could not understand down to the score of Magic and evil spirits was the usual custom of the blacks; but this time it seemed more than usually likely to be true. The Meki-gar, or medicine-men, nodded wisely, and the women all shuddered and wailed afresh, while the men looked anxious and afraid. Burkamukk thought for a moment before replying. He was a very wise chief, and while he was just as afraid of Magic as any other blackfellow, still he had the safety of his tribe to consider.

"That is all very well," he said, at length. "Very likely it is true. But it may not be true after all: Kuperee may be no more than a very wonderful kangaroo who has managed to grow to an enormous size. If that is so, he will want much food, and gradually he will hunt farther and farther, all over the country, until at last he will come here. Then we shall all suffer."

"Ay," said the men. "That is true. But what can we do?"

"I will not sit down quietly until I know for certain that Kuperee is Magic," said Burkamukk, striking the ground with the butt of his eel-spear. "If indeed he be Magic, then it will be the part of the Meki-gar to deal with him. But first I would have my young men prove whether they cannot avenge Kon-garn. It is in my mind that this Kuperee is no more than a huge animal; and I want his blood. Who will shed it for me?"

There was no lack of brave warriors among the men of Burkamukk. A shout went up from them, and immediately forty or fifty sprang before him, waking all the Bush echoes with their yells of defiance against Kuperee or any other giant animal, whether kangaroo or anything else. Only Tullum and the hunters who had been with him hung back; and they were unnoticed in the general excitement.

"Ye are too many," Burkamukk said, surveying them proudly. "Ten such men should be a match for any kangaroo." He ran his eye over them rapidly and counted out half a score by name. Then he bade the other volunteers fall back, so that the chosen warriors were left standing alone.

"It is well," he said. "Namba shall be your leader, and you will obey him in all things. Find out from Tullum where to look for this Kuperee, and see that you go warily, and that your weapons are always ready. Go; seek Kuperee, and ere seven sleeps have gone, bring me his tail to eat!" He stalked towards his wurley. The young men, shouting yells of battle, rushed for their weapons. In ten minutes they had gone, running swiftly over the plain, and the camp was quiet again, save for the cries of Kon-garn's wife as she mourned for her husband.

But alas! within a few days the wife of Kon-garn was not the only woman to bewail her dead. In less than a week the hunting-party was back, and without three of its bravest warriors. The survivors told the same story as Tullum and his men. They had found Kuperee, this time roaming through the Bush in search of food; and he had uttered a roar and rushed upon them. They had fought, they said, but unavailingly: spears and throwing-sticks seemed to fall back blunted from the monster's hide, and two of the men had been seized and devoured, while the third, Namba, who rushed wildly in, frantically endeavouring to save them, had been crushed to earth with one sweeping blow. Then terror, overwhelming and unconquerable, had fallen on the seven men who remained, and they had fled, never stopping until they were far away. Weaponless and ashamed, they crept back to the camp with their miserable story.

Burkamukk heard them in silence. Other chiefs might have been angry, and inflicted fierce punishments, but he knew that to such men there could be no heavier penalty than to return beaten and afraid. He nodded, when they had finished.

"Then it would surely seem that Kuperee is Magic," he said. "Therefore no man can deal with him, save only the medicine-men. Go to your wurleys and rest."

The Meki-gar were not at all anxious for the task of ridding the earth of Kuperee, but since their art, like that of all medicine-men, consisted in saying as little as possible, they dared not show their disinclination. Instead, they accepted Burkamukk's instructions in owl-like silence, making themselves look as wise as possible, and nodding as though giant kangaroos came their way—and were swept out of it—every day in the week. Then they withdrew to a lonely place outside their camp and began their spells. They lit tiny fires and burned scraps of kangaroo-hide, throwing the ashes in the air and uttering terrible curses against Kuperee. Also they secretly weaved many magic spells, sitting by their little fires and keeping a sharp look-out lest any of the tribe should see what they were doing—an unnecessary precaution, since the tribe was far too terrified of Magic to go anywhere near them. When they had been at work for what they considered a sufficient length of time, they packed up all their charms in skin bags, and returned to the camp, where they told Burkamukk that Kuperee was probably dead, as a result of their incantations. "But if he is not," said their head man, "then it is because we have nothing belonging to Kuperee himself to make spells with. If we had so much of a hair of his tail, or even one of the bones that he has gnawed, then we could make such a spell that nothing in the world could stand against it. As it is, we have done wonderful things, and he is very likely dead. Certainly no other Meki-gar could have done as much."

Burkamukk thanked the Meki-gar very respectfully. He did not understand their Magic at all, and he was badly afraid of all Magic; still, he knew that the Meki-gar did not always succeed in their undertakings, and he felt that though their spells were, no doubt, strong, there was quite a chance that Kuperee was stronger. He would have felt much happier had the Meki-gar been able to prove that the enemy was dead. "If I could give them a hair of his tail," thought he, "there would be no need for spells, since Kuperee will certainly be dead before he allows anyone to meddle with his tail." It was with some bitterness that he dismissed the wise men, giving them a present of roasted wallaby.

It was not long before proof came that the Magic of the Meki-gar had been at fault. Burkamukk's young men, out hunting, met a hunting-party of a friendly tribe, from whom they learned that the great kangaroo was fiercer and more powerful than ever, and had slain many men in the country to the north. As Burkamukk had foreseen, he was ranging farther and farther afield, so that no district could feel safe from him. It could be only a question of time before Kuperee would wander down to his country.

Burkamukk held a council of war that night, at which all the warriors and the Meki-gar were present. The chief wanted to lead his best men against the monster, but the Meki-gar opposed the suggestion vigorously, saying that it was not right for the head of the tribe to run into a danger such as this. An ordinary battle was all very well, but this was Magic, and against it chiefs were just as ordinary men: and where would the tribe be without its mighty head? The warriors supported the Meki-gar, and they all argued about it until Burkamukk was ready to lose his temper. He had no wish to see his best hunters grow fewer and fewer—already two expeditions had ended in disaster and loss. The discussion was becoming an angry one when suddenly the chief's two eldest sons, Inda and Pilla, rose and spoke. They were young men, but already they were renowned hunters, famous at tracking and killing game: and besides their skill with weapons, it was said that they had learned from the Meki-gar much wisdom beyond the knowledge of ordinary men. Straight and tall as young rushes, they faced their father.

"Let us go," Inda said—"Pilla and I. Numbers are useless against Kuperee; it is only cunning that will slay him, and for that two men are better than a score. Give us a trial, and if we fail, then will be time enough to talk of a great expedition."

The chief looked at them with angry unhappiness.

"And if you fail?" he said. "Then I shall have lost my sons."

"What of that?" asked Pilla. "You have other sons, and we will have died for the tribe. That is the right of a chief's son. Other men's sons have tried, and some of them have died. Now it is our turn."

A murmur of dissent ran round the circle, for Pilla and Inda were much loved; and they were very young. But Burkamukk looked at them proudly, though his face was very sad.

"They say rightly," he said. "They are the chief's sons, and it is their privilege, if need be, to die for the tribe. Go, then, my sons, and may Pund-jel make your hearts cunning and your aim steady when you meet Kuperee."

"There is one thing we desire," Inda said. "Will you lend us your stone axe, my father? It seems to us that Kuperee will fall to no ordinary weapon, and a dream has come to us that bids us take the axe. But that is for you to say. It is a great thing to ask; but if we live we will bring it back to you in safety."

Burkamukk signed to a young man who stood near him, and bade him fetch the axe from his wurley. When it came, he handed it to his sons.

"It is a great treasure, but you are my sons, and you are worthy to bear it," he said. "Never before has it left my sight in the hands of any warrior, and I would that I were the one to wield it against Kuperee. Good luck go with it and with you, my sons!"

So Inda and Pilla made themselves ready to go, preparing as if they were to take part in a splendid corroboree. They painted themselves with white stripes, and over and under their eyes and on their cheeks drew streaks of red ochre. Round their heads they wore twisted bands of fur, and in these bands they stuck plumes, made of the white quill feathers of a black swan's wing. Kangaroo teeth were fastened in their hair, and necklaces of the same teeth hung down upon their breasts. From their shoulders hung the tails of yellow dingos. They wore belts and aprons of wallaby skin, and, fastened behind to these belts, stiff upright tufts of the neck feathers of the emu, like the tail of a cock. They bore many weapons, and each took it in turn to carry the stone axe of Burkamukk. The whole tribe came out to watch them go, and while the men were envious, the women wailed sadly, for they were young, and it seemed that they were going forth to die.

Chapter II

PILLA AND INDA TRAVELLED SWIFTLY through the Bush for the first two days of their journey. They passed through good hunting country, where they were tempted by the sign of much game, but they would not allow themselves to turn aside, greatly as they longed for fresh meat. They carried a little food with them, and were fortunate in finding much boombul, which the white people afterwards called manna—a sweet white substance rather like small pieces of loaf-sugar, with a very delicate flavour. Boombul drops from the leaves and small branches of some kinds of gum-trees, and the blacks loved to eat it, so Pilla and Inda thought themselves very lucky.

They met friendly blacks now and then, as they travelled, and heard many stories of the ferocity of Kuperee. Some of the reports were very terrifying. It was difficult to find out how huge he was, for he seemed to grow in size according to the terror of the men who had seen him: some of whom said he was as large as any gum-tree. But all were agreed as to his fierceness. He devoured men in a single gulp: he struck them down as one might strike a yurkurn, or lizard: his swiftness in pursuit was terrible to see. The man he chased had no chance whatever, unless he managed to reach thick timber, where Kuperee's size prevented his taking the gigantic leaps which so quickly ended a chase on open ground. And about all the tales hung the sense of blind fear which the great beast seemed to inspire. No matter how brave a fighting-man might be, the sight of Kuperee seemed to turn his heart to water, making him long only to flee like a frightened child. Their voices shook with terror as they spoke of him.

"It seems to me," said Inda, as they journeyed on, after having talked to some of these hunters, "that our first thought should be for ourselves. All these men have thought themselves very brave, and have gone out to meet Kuperee, never doubting that they would not be afraid: and they have become very afraid indeed. Now you and I are no cowards in ordinary fighting, and we have had no fear of ourselves. But I think we had better make up our minds that we certainly shall become afraid, and decide what to do. I do not wish to lose my senses and run away like a beaten pickaninny."

"That is good sense," said Pilla. "Perhaps if we managed to keep our heads during our first terror it might pass after a time, so that we should again be as men."

"That is my idea," Inda answered. "And if Kuperee did not happen to see us while we were afraid, so much the better for us. I do not believe that fear will be with us always, but still, we are no better than all these other men. I believe we will get an attack of it, and then it will pass off, like an attack of sickness, if we treat it properly."

"Yes," said Pilla, nodding. "But if we run away we shall be afraid for ever—always supposing we are not dead."

"If we run away, the one that Kuperee runs after will certainly be

MARY GRANT BRUCE

dead," Inda said. "Therefore, let us go very warily, and perhaps we can manage so that he does not see us during our first fear."

"It is a queer thing," Pilla said, laughing, "for hunters to go out making certain of being afraid."

"I think it is a safe thing just now," said Inda shortly. "This hunting is not like other hunting."

So they went on, keeping a very sharp look-out, and having their weapons always ready. The stone axe of Burkamukk was rather troublesome to them, for their hands were encumbered with spears and throwing-sticks, and they were not used to carrying an axe: so, at last, Inda twisted strings of bark and slung it across his shoulders, where it felt much more comfortable. Soon they came upon traces of the great beast they sought. The forest began to be full of his tracks, and the saplings had been pulled about and gnawed by some creature larger than anything they had ever seen. And then, one evening, they heard running feet, and, leaping to one side, spear in hand, they saw half a dozen men, racing through the Bush, blind with terror. One slipped and fell near where they were standing, and rolled almost to their feet. Pilla and Inda drew him into a thicket.

"Is Kuperee after you?" they asked.

The man rolled his eyes upwards.

"He has slain two of us, and is now in pursuit of us all," he panted. "Let me go!" He scrambled to his feet and dashed away.

Pilla and Inda crouched low in the thicket, seeing nothing. But presently they heard a mighty pounding through the trees fifty yards away: and though nothing was visible, the sound of those great leaps was so terrifying in itself that they found themselves trembling. The pounding died away in the direction in which the blacks had gone.

"Ky! what a tail he must have, that makes the earth shake as he goes!" Inda muttered. "Never have I heard anything like it! Art afraid, Pilla?"

"Very much, I believe," said Pilla. "But it will pass, I feel sure. Brother, it seems to me that Kuperee's den must be not far off, and it would be safe to try to find it, since he has gone southward for his hunting: and most likely he will return slowly. Let us push on, while we can go quickly."

"That is good talk," Inda answered. "Perhaps we can hide ourselves near his den, and watch him without being seen. I should like to get my terror over in a high tree."

"I, too," said Pilla. "I fancy the attack might pass more quickly. Let us hurry."

They pushed onward as fast as possible. It was not hard to find the way, for the blacks had fled too madly to trouble about leaving tracks, and the marks of their running made a clear path, to native eyes. Soon, too, they came upon Kuperee's tracks—great footprints and deep depressions in the earth where his enormous tail had hit the ground at every bound. Then the Bush became more and more beaten down, as though some great animal roamed through it constantly; and at last they found the body of a hunter, struck down from behind as he ran.

"It was no playful tap that killed him," said Pilla, with a shudder. "The other, I suppose, was eaten as Kuperee loves to eat men, in one gulp. See, Inda—is not that where he sleeps?"

They were near a cleared space, where the ground was much trampled. Bones lay here and there, and in the shadow of a dense lightwood tree in the middle the grass showed clearly where a great body had often lain. No kangaroo has any kind of hole, for they love the Bush to sleep in, and Kuperee was evidently like other kangaroos in this. Probably he changed his home often; but this was a good place, ringed about with bushes that made it quiet and hard to find, so that no enemy was likely to come upon him too suddenly; while, from his lair under the lightwood, he could see anything approach.

"Men, or animals, or leaves—it does not seem to matter to him what he eats," said Inda, looking at the lair. "No wonder he grows huge. Pilla, I am very afraid, but I feel I will not always be afraid. Let us climb up into the lightwood tree; he will never see us among its thick leaves. Then he will come home tired, and perhaps we can spear him as he sleeps."

They climbed up into the dense branches, mounting high, and choosing stout limbs to lie on where they could peer down below; and they fixed their spears and other weapons so that they could use them easily. The stone axe of Burkamukk was much in Inda's way in climbing, and finally he untied it from his shoulders.

"I do not see how I can use this in the tree," he said. "See, I will strike it into the trunk, so that we can get at it handily if we need it."

He smote it against the trunk, and the wood held it fast. Then he and Pilla took their places, and watched for the coming of Kuperee.

They had not long to wait. Presently came, far off, the sound of great bounds and breaking saplings; not, as they had heard it last, in

MARY GRANT BRUCE

the fierceness of pursuit, but slowly, as a man may return home after successful hunting. The brothers felt their hearts thumping as they waited. Nearer and nearer came the sound, and soon the bushes parted and a mighty kangaroo hopped into the clearing.

So huge was he, so black and fierce, that they caught at each other in terror. Never had they dreamed of any kangaroo like this. His fur was thick and long, and of a glossy black; his head carried proudly aloft, his great tail like the limb of a tree. And in his gleaming eyes, and on his fierce face, was an expression of cunning and ferocity that, even more than his size, made him unlike any animal the Bush had ever known. Something of mystery and terror seemed to surround him; it was indeed clear that he was Magic. Pilla and Inda trembled so that they feared that the lightwood would shake and reveal them to the monster.

He sat down, out on the clear space, and rubbed his mouth with his forepaws, sniffing at the air so that they fell into a further terror, thinking he had smelt them out. But one blackfellow smells much like another, and Kuperee had recently dealt with three blacks: if he noticed any unusual odour he put it down to his late meal. He felt sleepy and well-fed; he had enjoyed both his run and his meal. Now, he only wanted sleep.

He hopped towards the lightwood, and at his coming Pilla and Inda felt themselves gripped by overmastering fear. Their teeth chattered; their dry tongues seemed to choke them. They clung to their boughs, dreading lest their trembling hold should loosen, bringing them tumbling at his feet. So, gripping with toes and fingers, with sweating cheeks pressed closely to the limbs, with staring eyes that peered downwards, they watched the dreadful beast come.

He came in under the tree and lay down, stretching himself out to sleep; and in a few moments his heavy breathing showed that he had passed quietly into slumber. As they watched, something of their terror left the brothers. Asleep, Kuperee was not so horrible; he looked, indeed, not so unlike any other kangaroo, with his fierce eyes veiled and the strength of his great body relaxed.

"I believe my time of fear is passing," Inda whispered. "He is but a kangaroo, after all."

"Yes, but what a terrible one!" murmured Pilla, as well as his chattering teeth would let him. "Still, we are mighty hunters, and no fools: unless he is really Magic we should be able to subdue him. I am beginning to feel a man again."

"We do not know for certain that he is Magic. Let us believe, then, that he is not, and that will help us," Inda whispered. "Why should we not spear him as he lies?"

"We might easily do it. Let us creep to the lower boughs, where we shall have more room to move our arms. Art afraid any longer, Inda?"

"Not as I was," Inda replied. "At least, not while he sleeps."

"Then let us try to arrange that he shall never wake," Pilla murmured.

Very softly, with infinite caution, they crept down the tree, until they came to the great lower limbs. Here they had space to swing their arms, and they made their weapons ready. Below, the huge kangaroo never stirred. His deep breathing, telling of sound slumber, was music in the ears of the brothers. They nodded a signal to each other as they poised their first spears.

So swiftly did they throw that before Kuperee was aroused from his sleep a shower of throwing-sticks and spears had hurtled through the air. Not one missed; the mark was easy, and the brothers were proved hunters. The weapons sped fast and true. But a terrible thing happened. Each point, as it struck Kuperee's fur, became blunt, and, instead of piercing him in fifty places, the weapons fell back from him, spent and useless.

With a groan of fear, the brothers grasped at the branches and swung themselves aloft. Below, Kuperee's roar of fury drowned all other sounds. He sprang to his feet, his eyes blazing. He had received no injury, but he had been touched—that in itself was an indignity he had never suffered before. With another earth-shaking roar he looked about for his foes.

To be attacked from the air was a new experience for Kuperee. All his other enemies had come upon him out of the Bush, and it never occurred to him, in his rage, to look upward, where the shaking of the branches would certainly have revealed the terrified Pilla and Inda. Instead, seeing nothing, Kuperee made sure that the trees concealed the attackers. He roared again, dreadfully, and bounded across the clearing. The Bush closed behind him, but the sky rang with the echo of his terrible voice and the thud of the leaps that carried him rapidly away.

Kuperee sleeping and Kuperee awake and angry were two very different beings, and with the first movement of the monster all their fear had come back to Pilla and Inda. As roar succeeded roar they became more and more weak with terror. Their grip on the boughs relaxed with the trembling of their hands, and even as Kuperee bounded away they lost their hold and tumbled bodily out of the tree.

It was not far to the ground, but Pilla happened to fall first, and Inda fell on top of him, and they managed to hurt each other a good deal. They were in that excited and over-wrought state when anything seems an injury, and each lost his temper.

"You did that on purpose!" Pilla said, striking at his brother. "Take that!"

"Would you!" said Inda, between his teeth. "I'll teach you to hit me!"

He stooped and picked up one of the throwing-sticks and flung it at his brother. It hit Pilla violently on the nose, and made him furiously angry. He gathered an armful of the fallen spears, and, running back, threw them at Inda so swiftly that there was no time to dodge. They hit him all over his body, and though they had all become blunt, they hurt very badly. The blood was streaming from Pilla's nose, and when he had thrown all his spears he stopped to wipe it off with a tuft of grass. The pause gave them time to think, and they stared at each other. Suddenly they burst out laughing.

"What fools we are!" they said.

"Yes, we are indeed fools," said Inda, rubbing his bruises. "Kuperee may be back at any moment, and here we will be found, fighting each other like a couple of stupid boys. I am sorry I hurt you, brother."

"You have certainly done that," said Pilla, caressing his nose gently. "There will be a dint down my nose for ever—the bone is broken, I think. Why don't you hit Kuperee as hard as that?"

"I will, if I get the chance," Inda said. "And you yourself are no child when it comes to throwing spears—a good thing for me that they were blunt. Yes, brother, we are the biggest fools in the Bush. Now what are we to do?"

"Save yourself!" screamed Pilla. "Here comes Kuperee!"

The great kangaroo came bounding back through the bushes, and the brothers, wild with terror, flung themselves at the lightwood tree. Up they went, but only just in time. Inda's heel was grazed by Kuperee's claw as he gained the safety of the lower branches. He climbed up swiftly, and, clinging together, they looked down at their foe.

"He cannot climb!" gasped Pilla.

"No, but he will have the tree down!" cried his brother.

Kuperee was flinging himself against the tree, until it rocked beneath the blows of his great body. Again and again came the dull thud as he drew himself back and came dashing against the trunk. Gradually it yielded, beginning to lean sidewards. Lower and lower it came, and Kuperee, rising high on his hind-legs and tail, clawed upward at Inda.

As the hunter, with a cry of despair, tried to pull himself higher, Pilla, leaning from an upper branch, thrust something into his hand.

"It is the stone axe of our father," he gasped. "Strike with it, brother!"

Inda grasped the handle, and smote downward with all his might. The keen edge of the stone caught Kuperee in the forehead, and sank into his head. He fell back, wrenching the axe from Inda's hand. One more terrific roar rent the air—a cry of pain and anger fearful to hear. Then, with a dull groan the monster sank sidewards to the grass. He was dead.

It was long before Pilla and Inda dared to quit the shelter of the leaning tree. They could scarcely believe that their enemy was dead, until they saw the mighty limbs stiffen, and beheld a crow perch, unmolested, on Kuperee's head. Then the brothers came down from the tree and clasped each other's hands.

"That was a good blow of yours," said Pilla.

"Ay, but it would never have been struck had you not put the axe into my hands," said Inda. "I had forgotten all about it. Our names will live long, brother."

"That will be agreeable, but I wish my nose were not so sore," said Pilla. "And your bruises—how are they?"

"Sore enough—but I had almost forgotten them. Ky, but I am hungry, Pilla!"

"I, too," said Pilla, looking with interest at the great dead body. "Well, at least we have plenty of food—Burkamukk said long ago that Kuperee should be enough for the whole tribe. Let us skin him carefully, for his hide will be a proud trophy to take back to our father—if we can but carry it."

"We shall eat him while it is drying," Inda said. "Then the skin will be lighter, and we shall be exceedingly strong. Come, brother—my hunger grows worse."

They fell to work on the huge carcass with their sharp skinning-knives, made of the thigh-bones of kangaroos. And then befel the most wonderful thing of all.

Chapter III

INDA AND PILLA TOOK OFF the black hide of Kuperee, and pegged it out carefully with sharp sticks. Then they came back to the body, and their eyes glistened with satisfaction. Meat is the best thing in the world to a blackfellow, and never before had either seen so much meat. It was almost staggering to think that it was theirs, and to be eaten. All they had feared and suffered became as nothing in the prospect of that tremendous feast.

"Yakai!" mourned Pilla. "We shall never finish it all before it goes bad, not though we eat day and night without ceasing—as I mean to do."

"And I also," agreed Inda. "Let us make ovens before we begin to cut him up—we shall waste less time that way. Some of him will certainly go bad, but we will do our best."

They were turning aside to gather sticks when Pilla suddenly caught at his brother's arm. He happened to seize a bruised part, and Inda was justly annoyed.

"Take care, blockhead!" he said, shaking him off roughly. "I ache all over—is it not enough for you?"

Pilla took no notice. He was staring at the skinned body of Kuperee, with eyes that were almost starting from his head.

"Look!" he gasped. "Look! He moves!"

Inda leaped to one side.

"Moves!" he uttered. "Are you mad?"

"I saw his side move," Pilla repeated. "See—there it is again!"

Something bulged under the stripped skin of the monster. The brothers leaped backward.

"But he is certainly dead," gasped Inda. "Have we not skinned him? Can a skinned animal move—even if he be Kuperee?"

"Let us leave him and go home," muttered Pilla. "He is very bad Magic."

But that was more than Inda could bring himself to do.

"Leave him!" he exclaimed. "Leave the most wonderful feast ever heard of in all the Bush! No, I will not. Magic or no Magic, he is dead, and I will see what moves."

He sprang forward, knife in hand, and with a quick movement slit open the body. Out popped a head—a black head, with fear and pain and bewilderment on its features. Inda sprang back, raising his knife to defend himself.

"Let me out!" begged the head. "It is horrible in here—no air, no light, nothing but dead men! Let me out, I say!"

"Are you Magic?" gasped Inda.

"Magic? I?" The wild eyes rolled in astonishment. "I am Kanalka, of the Crow Tribe, But an hour ago Kuperee swallowed me at a gulp, when he came upon me in the forest. I do not know why I am not dead—but I live yet, though I was wishing to die when suddenly you let the light in to my prison. Make your hole larger, friend, and let me out."

"Do you say there are dead men there?" demanded Pilla.

"He is full of them. I only am alive, I suppose because I was the last eaten. Be quick! be quick!"

Half doubting, half afraid, Inda opened the great body, and helped Kanalka out. He staggered and fell helplessly to the ground. Pilla and Inda did not trouble about him. One after another, they took from Kuperee ten black hunters, laying them in a row upon the grass. Last of all they took out Kon-garn and three others of their own tribe, and they wailed over them.

Kanalka, who had somewhat recovered, came and looked curiously at the row of men.

"Would you not say that they were alive?" he asked. "They do not look as though they were anything but asleep."

"I think it is Magic," said Inda, very much afraid. "Two moons have gone by since Kon-garn, who lies there, was eaten, and yet he looks as though asleep. Kuperee was a strange host, truly, to keep you all in such good condition!"

The gaze of Kanalka wandered to the stone axe of Burkamukk, which lay on the grass near Kuperee. Instantly he became interested. He had seen many dead men, but no such axe as this had come his way.

"Is that the mighty axe of which all the tribes have heard?" he asked eagerly. "Ky! what a beauty! Never have I seen such a one! I should like to handle it."

He picked it up and tested its weight, while Pilla and Inda watched him carefully, for they knew that the axe was a treasure beyond anything in the Bush, and that a man would risk almost anything to possess it. They need not, however, have feared Kanalka. He was a simple-minded fellow, and was merely lost in admiration.

"A beauty, indeed!" he exclaimed. "It will be something to tell my people, that in the one day I escaped from the body of Kuperee and handled the stone axe of Burkamukk! Was it with this that you killed the monster?"

"Ay," said Inda. "It clove his skull—one blow was enough, though our spears had fallen blunted from his hide."

"A marvel, indeed!" cried Kanalka. "It would be a mighty weapon at close quarters in a fight. One would swing it round—thus—and bring it down upon the enemy's head—"

He illustrated his meaning, swinging the axe aloft and bringing it down over the head of the silent form of Kon-garn. Just before it reached the head he checked it, letting it do no more than touch Kon-garn—a touch no heavier than the sweep of a butterfly's wing.

Kon-garn yawned, sneezed, and sat up.

With a yell of terror the three blacks started backwards, tripped over each other, and fell in a heap. Kon-garn surveyed the struggling mass calmly.

"Where am I?" he asked. "And what is all this about? Is it you, Pilla and Inda?"

They struggled to their feet and looked at him distrustfully.

"You are dead," said Pilla firmly. "Why do you talk?"

"I do not know why, indeed, since it is evident that I am talking to fools," said Kon-garn rudely. "What has happened to you, that you and this stranger have suddenly gone mad? Ky! how hungry I am! Have you food?"

The brothers suddenly began to laugh helplessly.

"Food!" said Inda. "There is more food than ever you saw before, Kon-garn, and a few minutes ago you were part of it."

"That is a riddle I am too tired to guess," said Kon-garn crossly. "I only wish that any food were part of me, for I feel as though I had never eaten in my life."

"It is certainly two moons at least since last you ate," Pilla told him.

"I said already that you were mad, and I grow more sure of it every minute," said poor Kon-garn. "Who are these who lie beside me?"

"They are dead men; and a moment ago you too were dead," Inda said.

Kon-garn became afraid, as well as cross. It was clear that everybody was mad, and he had heard that it was wise to humour mad people, or they might do you an injury. So he hid his feelings and looked at the brothers as kindly as his bewilderment and hunger would let him.

"Dead, was I?" he said. "Then how did I come to life?"

"This man touched you with the stone axe of Burkamukk," Inda answered.

"Dear me, how simple!" said Kon-garn. "None of our Meki-gar know anything half so easy. But why does he not go on, and bring all these other dead men to life too?"

"Indeed," said Kanalka suddenly, "I do not know."

He flung himself upon the stone axe, which he had let fall in his terror, and touched another still form with it. Instantly the black hunter came to life. Kanalka uttered a wild yell of amazement and triumph. Then Inda snatched the axe from him and ran along the line, touching one man after another; and when he had come to the end there were ten blackfellows sitting up and rubbing their eyes, and most of them were asking eagerly for food. The brothers drew back a few paces and looked at them.

"It is clear," said Pilla, "that Kuperee was Magic, and that when our father's stone axe entered his skull it became Magic too. More than ever we must guard it carefully, since it seems to have the power of life and death." He lowered his voice, speaking to Inda. "I will lash it to your shoulders, brother—we are among strangers, and it will be safer so."

He lashed the axe to Inda's shoulders firmly, and the other men looked on. Each knew exactly why he was doing it, and respected him for his caution, since each knew that had chance thrown in his way the mighty stone axe he would not have been proof against the temptation of trying to get possession of it. Then they all talked together, and were very amazed at what had happened to them; but since they were able to put everything down to Magic, nothing worried them much, and they were quite relieved to find themselves alive, and to think of seeing their wives and children again. More than anything, they were overjoyed at the magnificent feast that awaited them.

And what a feast it was! Never again in all their lives did such a chance come to them. The wild black never asked for any trimmings with his food: he would, indeed, eat anything that came his way, but meat, meat only, and still more meat, was what his soul most desired. And now meat awaited them, in a huge mountain; and they were hungry beyond belief.

"We will cut up Kuperee," said Pilla and Inda, "since we alone have knives. The rest of you must make fire, and prepare ovens."

The men scattered to their tasks. Some gathered sticks; others scooped out holes in the ground for the ovens; others teased dry messmate bark for tinder for the man who was making the fire. This was Kon-garn, and he did it very quickly. Pilla lent him one of his most useful household necessaries, which he always carried with him—a piece of dry grass-tree cane, having a hole bored through to the pith on its upper side, and a pointed piece of soft wood; and these were just as useful to the blacks as a box of matches would be to you. Kon-garn sat down on the ground, holding the bit of grass-tree firmly down with his feet, and pressed the point of the soft wood into the little hole. Then he held it upright between his palms and twirled it rapidly. Within two minutes smoke began to curl round the twirling point, and another man carefully put some teased bark, soft and dry, round the hole and blew on it. A moment more and a thin tongue of flame licked through the tinder; more and more was fed to it, and then leaves and twigs; and in five minutes there was a blazing fire, while Kon-garn restored to Pilla his two flame-making sticks, very little the worse for wear.

The blacks did not usually light a large fire, after the fashion of white men, who like to make a campfire so big that they roast their faces while their backs remain cold. The way the blacks preferred was to make two little fires, and to sit between them, so that they were kept warm on both sides. But on this occasion they made a very big blaze, so that they should quickly have enough fire to heat the ovens; and then they made the big fire long and narrow, so that they could sit on each side of it and cook. While the ovens were getting hot they took small pieces of the Kangaroo meat and speared them on green sticks, holding them before the coals. They were all so desperately hungry that they did not care much whether the meat was properly cooked—as soon as the first pieces were warmed through they stuffed them into their mouths, and then ran to Pilla and Inda for more. Pilla and Inda were working hard at cutting up Kuperee, and though they did not mind the hungry men beginning without them, they became annoyed when they came again and again for fragments.

"Do not forget that we are hungry too," Pilla growled. "We have travelled far before we killed Kuperee and let you all out, and now we are cutting up your meat for you. If you do not bring us some cooked pieces we must go and cook for ourselves."

That made the others afraid, for the cutting-up of so huge an animal as Kuperee was no light work, and none of them had knives. So they fed the brothers with toothsome morsels as they worked, and the cutting went on unchecked, until the ovens were hot and there was a pile of joints ready to be put in. This was done, wrapping the joints in green leaves. Then they carried to the fire the great heap of small pieces of meat left from the cutting-up, and cooked and ate, and ate and cooked, all through the night.

Even in ordinary life it would have astonished you to see how much meat a black could eat—a well-fed blackfellow, with a wife who kept his wurley well supplied with roots and grubs and all the other pleasant things they loved. But these blacks had had no food, some of them for weeks, and it seemed that they would never stop. The great pile of pieces dwindled until there were none left, and then they hacked more off, and cooked and ate until the ovens were ready and the smoking joints came out. They were so hot that you would not have cared to touch them without a knife and fork; but the blacks seized them and tore them to pieces and gnawed them, until nothing remained but well-picked bones. And then they cooked more.

Pilla and Inda were the first to give in, and they had eaten enough for twenty white men. They waddled off to a thicket and flung themselves under a bush, sleeping back to back, so that the stone axe of Burkamukk was safe between them. But the others had no thought for anything but Kangaroo, and even the mighty axe could not have tempted them from that tremendous gorge. They ate on, all through the day. Towards night some of them gave in; then, one by one, they could eat no more, and most of them went to sleep where they sat before the fire. But dawn on the next day showed the steadfast Kon-garn, rotund beyond belief, and eating still. And by that time Pilla and Inda had slept off their light repast, and were ready to begin all over again.

They camped for more than a week by the carcass of Kuperee, and ate it until it was no longer pleasant to eat, even for a blackfellow. Then they began to think it was time to return to their tribes. So they greased their bodies comfortably all over, and set off through the forest, a peaceful and happy band, far too well-fed to think of quarrelling. When they came near the head-quarters of each tribe they marched to its camp in a proud procession, returning the warriors who had been mourned as dead: and great were the rejoicings throughout the country, and rich rewards of furs and weapons and food were showered upon Inda and Pilla. The stone axe of Burkamukk became more famous than ever, and everyone wanted to look at the wonderful weapon that had slain Kuperee. Songs were made about the two heroes, and for ages afterwards mothers used to tell their children about them, and hope that their boys would be as brave as Burkamukk's sons.

At last they drew near to their own camp. They halted the night before a few hours' journey away, and by good luck they met a couple of boys out hunting, and sent them in to tell the tribe that they were coming. They had no idea of coming in unheralded, for they knew they had done a great deed, and they meant to return in state. Besides, although the rescued men were with them, the load of presents they had received was far too heavy to be carried comfortably.

They got up early and painted themselves in stripes and put on their finest feathers and furs. Inda carried the stone axe of Burkamukk, and Pilla had only a spear. Long before they were ready to start they were met by some of the men of the tribe who had come out to welcome them. These loaded themselves with the gifts, and with Pilla and Inda stalking in front, and the rescued men behind, they formed themselves into a procession and marched for home.

Near the camp another procession came out to meet them: Burkamukk, their father, marching at the head of all his tribe. First came the Meki-gar, very solemn, and inwardly very disgusted that the honour of slaying Kuperee had not fallen to them; then came all the warriors and the old men, then the boys, and lastly the women and children. They were shouting greetings and praises and singing songs of welcome. Burkamukk halted as his sons drew near. They came up to him and knelt before him and Inda laid the stone axe at his feet.

"We bring you back your mighty weapon, my father," he said. "It has slain your enemy."

Then all the tribe shouted afresh, and the warriors leaped in the air, and the whole country was filled with the sound of their rejoicings. And they bore Pilla and Inda home in triumph, naming them the most famous heroes of all the tribes of the Bush.

But the Magic of Kuperee was not done with them yet.

They feasted late that night, and the sun was high overhead before they woke next day. They were in a wurley by themselves, but outside the boys of the tribe were clustered, peeping in to see the mighty warriors. Pilla stretched himself, and flung out an arm, which struck Inda.

"Take care!" Inda said, angrily, waking up. "You hurt me."

"Why, I hardly touched you," Pilla answered. "You must have been dreaming."

"Well, it is no dream that I am very sore," said Inda. "All my body seems covered with bruises, just as it was after our fight under the tree of Kuperee."

"That is queer," said Pilla, "for my nose also feels terribly sore. That must have been a mighty blow that you dealt it." He felt it tenderly. "It feels queer, too. Does it look curious?"

"There is a furrow down it, but then there always has been, since our fight," said Inda. "You look not much worse than usual. But I—see, is there anything wrong with me?"

He flung off his wallaby-skin rug, and sat up. Pilla uttered a cry.

"Ky! you are all over spots! Did I really hit you in all those places?"

"You must have done so," said Inda, crossly. "Lucky for me that the spears were blunt!"

"I feel most extraordinary," said Pilla, suddenly "It is just as though I were shrinking—and indeed, I have no cause to shrink, seeing how much I ate last night. But my skin is getting all loose."

"And mine too!" cried Inda, faintly. "There is Magic at work upon us, my brother!"

Then a mist drifted over the wurley, and strange cries came out of it. The boys, watching outside, clutched at each other in fear. And presently, when the mist blew away, Pilla and Inda were not to be seen, nor were they ever seen more. Instead, within the wurley crouched two little animals, new to the blacks, which uttered faint squeaks and scurried away through the camp into the Bush.

There they live now, and through them are the sons of Burkamukk remembered. Pilla is the plump 'possum, who has always a furrow down his nose; and Inda is the native-cat, whose skin is covered all over with spots. For the Magic of Kuperee lived after him, so that the blunt weapons that had struck him had strange power, just as there was power of life in the stone axe that had killed him. But though they lived no longer as men, the names of Pilla and Inda were always held in great honour, since through their courage and wisdom the tribes lived in security, free from the wickedness of Kuperee.

II

Waung, the Crow

Chapter I

VERY LONG AGO—SO LONG that the oldest blacks could not remember anything about it themselves—there was a legend of the first coming of Fire.

Fire came with a group of seven strange women, the Kar-ak-ar-ook, who brought it from some unknown country. They dwelt with the blacks, and showed them how to use the new and wonderful thing: but they were very selfish, and would give none away. Instead, they kept it in the end of their yam-sticks, and when the people begged for it, they only laughed at them. They alone knew how to make it, and they never told the secret to anyone.

So the blacks took counsel together.

"We might as well have never learned that there was Fire at all," said one.

"Better," said another. "Before it came, we were content: but now, everyone is sighing for it, and cannot get it."

"My wife is a weariness to me," said a third. "Always she pesters me to bring Fire to her, and makes my mouth water by telling me of the beautiful food she could cook if she had it. It is almost enough to make a man lose his appetite!"

"But who that has once tasted cooked food can ever forget it?" another said, licking his lips. "Such flavour! Such juiciness! Twice the Kar-ak-ar-ook gave Fire to my wife, and let her roast wallaby and snipe—and since those glorious meals it is hard to eat them raw."

"Ay, that is so," said one. "To my woman also, they gave Fire twice, and she cooked me wombat and iguana. Ky! how much I ate, and how sick I was afterwards! But it was worth it."

"And fish!" said another. "No one who eats raw fish can imagine what a difference Fire makes to it. It is indeed a wonderful thing. The first time I saw it, I picked it up, admiring its pretty colour, and it stung me severely. In my wrath I kicked it, but its sting was still there, and it gave me a very sore foot. Now I know that it is Magic, and must not be touched, save with a stick—and then the stick becomes part of it. It is all very curious."

"It is worse than curious that such a thing should be, and be held only by the power of women," said an old man, angrily. "If we had fire, the winter cold would not strike so keenly to old bones. Why should we submit to these women, the Kar-ak-ar-ook? Let us kill them, if necessary, and take it from them for ourselves."

But no one moved, and all looked uneasy.

"The women are Magic," said one, at length. "The magic-men know that."

"Yes, and the women's Magic is stronger than theirs," another answered. "They have weaved spells, but what good have they done?"

"Now, they say that unless they let some Fire drop by accident, we can never get it from them: and if they do let it fall, then they will be just like other women, and have no power at all. I would like to see that!" said a big fellow, eagerly. "It would be very good for them, and they would make useful wives for some of us, for they know all about cooking food. I would not mind marrying one of them myself!" he added, in a patronizing tone, at which everybody laughed.

Another big man spoke. His name was Waung, and he was tall and powerful.

"It is all very ridiculous," he said. "No woman lives in the world who can get the better of a man. I have half a mind to get Fire from them myself."

"You!" said the others, and they all joined in roars of laughter. For Waung was a lazy man, and had never done much good for himself. "You! You would go to sleep instead of finding a way to get the better of the Kar-ak-ar-ook!"

This made Waung very angry.

"You are all fools!" he said, rudely. "I will certainly take the trouble to get Fire, and will make one of the women my wife, and she shall cook in my wurley. But then I will have their Magic, and none of you will get any Fire from me, of that you may be sure. Then you will all be sorry!" But this only made the men laugh more, and the noise of their mirth set the laughing-jackasses shouting in the trees. Very seldom had the camp heard so fine a joke.

Waung was filled with fury. He strode away from them, with his head in the air, shouting fierce threats. No one took the least notice of them, because he was known to be a boaster and a talker; but it was very amusing to see him go, and the blacks were always glad of a chance for laughter. Even after Waung had gone into his wurley, he could hear the echo of their merriment; and whenever two or three went past, they were still talking about him and laughing. "A pity Waung is such a fool!" they said. "But perhaps it is as well, for if there were no fools we would not have such good jokes!" And that did not make Waung feel any better.

Next day he went to the Kar-ak-ar-ook's wurley, and met them going out to dig for yams. Their dilly-bags were on their shoulders; and they held their yam-sticks, and he could see Fire gleaming in the hollow tops. Waung looked at the digging ends of the sticks, and saw that they were very blunt. He said: "I will sharpen your yam-sticks for you."

The Kar-ak-ar-ook thanked him, with a twinkle in their eyes. They knew there was some reason for such politeness from Waung. So they held the yam-sticks for him to cut, and though once or twice he tried to make them fall, as if by accident, so long as they had even a finger upon them they did not move. So Waung realized that Fire was not to be obtained in that way. When he had finished the points, he stood up.

"I am sick of the tribe," he said, angrily. "They are silly people, and they turn me into a joke. If you like, I will come out and help you to get food—and, I can tell you, I know where to hunt. Will you hunt with me?"

Now the Kar-ak-ar-ook were suspicious of Waung, but they were lazy women. It did not amuse them at all to go hunting by themselves every day, for they were not clever at it, and it took them a long time to find enough game to cook. Moreover, they were fond of food, and never had enough. They knew that no one could take away their yam-sticks so long as they held them; and so they were not afraid of Waung.

"Perhaps what you say is true," one answered slowly. "At any rate, I do not care. You may come with me if you wish, and sometimes we will give you some cooked food."

So the camp got used to the sight of Waung and the women going out to hunt together; and after a while they forgot that they used to laugh at them, and they had to find another joke. They envied Waung very much if they saw him eating scraps of cooked meat given him by the women: and you may be sure that Waung did not give any scraps away. He became quite good friends with the women, though they were always suspicious of him, and gave him no chance of handling their yam-sticks. The fire in the hollow tops never went out. Waung could not guess how they managed to keep it alive there, and it puzzled him very much. But he never forgot that he had vowed to take it from them, and he made many plans that came to nothing, because the Kar-ak-ar-ook were always watchful.

At last Waung hit upon an idea. Out in the scrub he found a nest of young snakes, and these he managed to tame, for he was a very cunning man. Even when they were nearly full-grown they would do his bidding, and he taught them many queer tricks. Then he went in search of an ant-hill, and sought until he found a very large one. For the Kar-ak-ar-ook had told him that they loved ants' eggs more than any kind of food.

One night, Waung took his snakes, and buried them in the ant-hill, saying, "Stay there until I send to let you out." They looked at him with their fierce, beady eyes, and wriggled round until they made themselves nests in the soft earth, which caused the ants very great inconvenience and alarm. Then Waung covered them up and went home, taking the Kar-ak-ar-ook a little kangaroo-rat that he had killed.

The women were hungry, and the sight of Waung's offering did not please them.

"It is very small," they said, discontentedly. "What is the matter with you? You have brought us scarcely any food for three days."

Waung laughed, swinging his spear.

"Hunting has been bad," he said, carelessly. "I have been lazy, perhaps—or the game was scarce. But I have a treat for you tomorrow."

"What is that?" they asked, eagerly, looking up from skinning the kangaroo-rat.

"What would you say to ants' eggs?"

"We like them more than anything else," they cried. "Have you found some?"

"I have found a very big hill," Waung said. "It should be full of eggs."

"And you will take us there?"

Waung did not want to seem too eager. He hesitated.

"I do not want the eggs," he said, at length. "A man wants something he can bite—eggs are for women. But will you cook me a wallaby if I take you there?"

"Where is the wallaby?" asked the Kar-ak-ar-ook.

"I have not caught it yet. But I have set a snare in a track I know— and while you dig ants' eggs I have no doubt I can get one. That does not matter, however—I can get one some time. Will you cook it for me, if I show you the ants' nest?"

The Kar-ak-ar-ook promised, for the temptation of the ants' eggs was very strong. They ate all the kangaroo-rat, and found it quite too small for their appetites: so they went to sleep hungry, and were still hungrier when they awoke in the morning. They had only a few yams for breakfast, and so they were very eager to start when Waung sauntered up to their wurley.

They all went a little way into the Bush, and then came upon the great ant-hill. At the sight, the Kar-ak-ar-ook ran forward, with their sticks ready to dig.

Waung said:

"I will go on to my snare, and come back to you."

But he went slowly. The women had not taken any notice of what he said. They plunged their yam-sticks into the hill, and began throwing out the earth quickly. Then they uttered a loud scream, for the snakes came tumbling out of the loosened earth and ran this way and that, hissing fiercely—and some ran at them.

Waung turned back at their cries.

"Hit them with your sticks!" he shouted. "Kill them."

The Kar-ak-ar-ook hit furiously at the snakes with the pointed end of their yam-sticks. But a stiff, pointed stick is not much use for killing snakes, as Waung well knew, and he called to them roughly:

"That is no good—use the thick ends!"

The women swung their sticks round at his cry, and brought the thick ends down across the snakes' backs. The blows were so strong that many of the snakes were killed at once—but that was not the only thing that happened. Fire flew out of the hollow ends of the sticks, and, in great coals, rolled down the side of the ant-hill. The coals met and joined, so that they were all one very large coal.

Waung had been watching like a cat. He had picked up two flat pieces of green stringy-bark; and now he leaped forward, snapped up Fire between them, and fled. Behind him came the Kar-ak-ar-ook, screaming. But as Waung stole the Fire, their Magic left them, and they were helpless.

Then Bellin-Bellin, the Musk-Crow, who carries the whirlwind in his bag, heard the voice of Pund-jel speaking to him out of the clouds, commanding him to let loose his burden. So Bellin-Bellin, obedient, but greatly afraid, untied the strings of his bag, and the whirlwind leapt out with a wild rush. It caught the Kar-ak-ar-ook, and whirled them up into the sky, where you may still see them, clustered together, for they were turned into stars. Now they are called the Pleiades, or Seven Sisters. But the blacks know that they are the Kar-ak-ar-ook women, and that they live together in the sky, still carrying Fire on the ends of their yam-sticks.

Chapter II

WAUNG WENT PROUDLY BACK TO the tribe, and when they saw that he had actually stolen Fire from the women, they were both glad and astonished, and clustered round him, calling him many pleasant things. Waung was quite ready to listen to them; but he had no intention of being generous now that he had brought Fire with him. He saw his way to a lazy life, and he was not the man to lose such a good chance.

So after they had praised him very loudly and sung loud songs about his bravery and wit, he went off into his wurley, and put Fire in a hole in the ground. Then he sat in the doorway and carved a boomerang.

The people looked at each other, not knowing what to do next.

"How is this?" they said. "Will he not give Fire to us all?"

No one could answer this question. They chattered together for a while. Then one said, "What is worth having is worth asking for"; and he went up to Waung's wurley and greeted him civilly.

"Good-day, Waung," he said. "Will you give me some fire to do my cooking?"

"I have only enough for myself," said Waung, and went on with his carving.

"But Fire grows, if you will let it," said the man. "Will you not make it grow, so that each of us may have some?"

"I cannot spare any," was all that Waung would answer. So the man went back to his friends, and told them what Waung said. Then one after another came to Waung, and begged him for a little bit of Fire. But the reply was always the same, and they went away, very sorry that they had ever laughed at Waung. For now he remembered the laughter, and he determined to have his revenge.

In the morning, when the tribe was astir they found that Waung had made a very large oven in front of his wurley, and had hid Fire there. Also he had caught a wallaby in his snare, and all the air was full of the fragrant smell of cooking. It made all the people's mouths water, and they hated Waung exceedingly. But they feared that with the Kar-ak-ar-ook's Fire Waung had also captured their Magic, and so they did not dare to attack him.

So they held a council together, and all talked very fast and angrily: but at the end of it, there was nothing accomplished. Talking did not mend the matter at all, and against Magic, what could anyone do? Then a woman came running, and said she had a message, and though women were not supposed to speak in council, she was told to deliver it at once.

"Waung says he will cook our food!" said she, and stopped for breath. A great shout of joy went up from the men.

"But he will not do it for nothing," went on the woman. At this all their faces lengthened suddenly. The blacks stopped in the middle of their joyful shout, and waited with their mouths wide open to hear what was to follow.

"He says he will cook for us. But we are to supply him with food, and firewood, and all that he wants, and he will keep for himself all the food he likes best. And if we do not perform all that he tells us to do, he will take Fire away altogether."

There was silence when the woman had finished speaking, and then a deep groan of anger went up from the people. They all talked very fast again, each trying to speak more loudly than the others, all except the husband of the woman who had brought the news, and he was busy beating her with his waddy because she had brought so insolent a message, and had allowed them to think at first that it was good news. The poor lubra tried to say that they had not given her time to say it all at once, but the husband was too busy to listen. But neither talking nor beating made the matter any better.

So Waung became the real ruler of the tribe, in everything but name, since food is the most important thing in the world to the blacks, and the greater part of their food became dependent upon him. Nothing could be cooked unless Waung would do it, and they soon found that unless he were in a good temper he would not do it at all. He took the best parts of all that they brought to him to cook, so that no man knew what he would get back; and when one took a fat young wallaby or a black duck it was quite likely that Waung would give him something tough and stringy when he went back for his cooked meal, declaring that it was what he had left in his oven. Neither would he take any trouble over the cooking. The people brought their food, and put it in the oven themselves, and Waung took it out when it pleased him.

Sometimes he did not take it out until it was burned black and tasteless, while at others they would find it only half-cooked, and cold. But no amount of talking would make Waung alter his ways, and at last he became so proud that if anyone argued with him he would refuse to cook for a week, except for himself. This naturally stopped all argument in the camp, but it did not make the people love Waung any better.

He grew very fat and lazy, for he ate huge quantities of food, and very seldom went out of his wurley. When he did, he carried Fire with him in a little hollow stick, and no one dared go near him, or near his wurley, for fear of his enchantments. As a matter of fact, Waung had no enchantments at all, and no Magic. But he was very cunning, and he knew how easy it was to make the blacks think he had amazing powers. The magic-men, too, found that none of their spells had any effect upon Waung, and so they told the tribe that he certainly had magic help. It was very convenient to be able to say this when they were beaten, for Magic was a thing that could not possibly be argued about.

The months went by, and the people became very unhappy. Waung's evil temper made them all miserable and afraid. There have been many bad kings in history, but only Waung ever had the power of depriving all his people of their dinner, if they failed to please him. It is a very terrible punishment when it is inflicted often, especially when dinner is the only meal of the day. Now that the people had grown used to cooked food, they did not like raw meat; so they depended on Waung's mercy. And Waung had very little mercy. It amused him greatly to see the people hungry and to have them come begging to him to cook their food. He would laugh loud and long, reminding them of the time when they had jeered at him about Fire. Afterwards, he would go into his wurley and sleep, saying, "Fire is asleep today, and I cannot wake it."

At last, Pund-jel, Maker of Men, looked down at the world and saw how unhappy the blacks were under the cruelties of Waung. It made him very angry. He was stern and hard himself, but he saw no reason why this fellow, lazy and ill-natured, should make his people hungry and miserable. So he sent a message to the ear of each man in the tribe, telling him what to do.

The blacks thought they had dreamed the message. They woke in the morning, confused and angry, they hardly knew why; and each man said to his neighbour, "I have dreamed about Waung," and the other would answer, "I, too, have dreamed about him." They gathered into groups, talking about Waung and about the dream that had come to them; and then the groups began to drift towards Waung's wurley.

Waung looked out, and saw them coming. At once he became uneasy, for he knew that he had never seen such threatening faces and angry eyes. It made him afraid, and he began to put Fire to heat his oven, which had been cold for five days.

The blacks came close to the wurley, growling and muttering. They circled round, still half-afraid. Then one, suddenly becoming brave, shouted a word of angry abuse at Waung; and that was all the others wanted. They joined the first man in loud and threatening shouts and fierce abuse, casting at him every evil name they could think of, and saying that the time had come for him to answer for his bad deeds. Then one picked up a stone and flung it at him, hitting him on the shoulder.

Waung had no weapons outside his wurley. He became terrified, gazing round him with hopeless eyes that saw no way of escape. Then he stooped to his oven, and saw that Fire lay there in a mass of red coals.

"I will give you back Fire!" he shouted.

He thrust a flat stone into the coals, and with it flung Fire far and wide among the blacks. Some of it hit the men and burned them, as he hoped, but others picked it up and ran with it to their wurleys, so that they might never again be without it in their homes. To and fro in the air the burning pieces flew as Waung hurled them from him. So fast they fell that the people were almost afraid again. It seemed as though Waung were making Fire, so that he might fight them with it.

And then a strange thing happened.

All the coals that had fallen in the dry grass nearest the wurley turned and began to burn back towards Waung. They met in a circle of flame. Gradually it burned until it came to the wurley, and there it wrapped Waung, and his oven, and all that belonged to him, in a sheet of flame. Out of it came Waung's dreadful cries for help; but no man dared go near the fire, nor would anyone have lifted a finger to help Waung.

The people huddled together, watching, in great fear. Soon the cries ceased, and then the smoke and flame died away, so that they saw the body of Waung, lying across the stones of his oven. He was quite black, like a cinder. The tribe uttered a long shout of triumph, for they knew that he could trouble them no more.

Then they heard the voice of Pund-jel, speaking to the thing that lay across the stones.

"Fire has made you black," said the voice. "Now you shall be black for ever, and no longer a man. Instead, you shall be a crow, to fly about for ever and utter cries, so that when the people see you they will remember how they were foolishly in bondage to you and your cruelties."

The people cast themselves down, in terror at the voice. A drifting cloud of smoke floated from the smouldering ashes of the wurley and blotted everything out.

When they looked again, it had lifted, and blown away into the skies. The thing that had lain on the stones was no longer there. But from the limb of a boobyalla tree close by came a harsh croak and, looking, they saw a big black crow that flapped its wings, and looked at them with sullen eyes. Then it said, "Waa-a-a! Waa-a-a-a!" and, rising from the tree, it flew lazily across to a great blackbutt, where it perched on the topmost bough, still croaking evilly. And the people, glad, yet afraid, clustered together, muttering, "See! It is Waung!"

III

The Emu who would Dance

Long ago, Kari, the Emu, was superior to all other birds. She was so superior that she would not live on the earth. Instead, she had a home up in the clouds, and from there she used to look down at the earth and the queer antics of all the things that lived there. It gave her much food for thought.

At that time there were no human beings at all. All the earth was inhabited by animals, birds, and reptiles, and they lived very happily together, as a rule. There were no wars, and everyone had enough to eat. While there were no men, Fear did not live on earth either. All the world was a big feeding-ground, where even the smallest and weakest could find a peaceful home.

Kari, sitting in her great nest up in the clouds, watched the animals below, both night and day. She thought them strange creatures, and wondered very much how they could be so contented with so many other creatures about them. She was so used to living alone that it seemed to her rather unpleasant to have one's solitude broken upon by others, all of whom might be peculiar enough to think their little affairs as interesting as one's own. Kari thought that nothing could possibly be so interesting as her great lonely nest in the clouds. In reality, it was a very dull old nest, and she was a big, dull bird. She knew no one, and spoke to no one, and thought only her own queer thoughts. But she did not know she was dull, and so she was quite happy.

One day she sat in her nest, watching the cloud-masses drift about between her and the world. They cleared away after a while, and she looked down upon a great forest over which she found herself, for, as her nest was in a cloud, it used to float about, and so she never knew what country she might see when she looked down. Sometimes it was a lake, sometimes a mountain, and sometimes the great, rolling sea, which always made her feel rather giddy, because it would not keep still for a moment.

But on this day it was a wide forest, green and peaceful. Kari's sight was very keen, and she looked through the tree-tops to the ground below and saw all the animals. It was really almost as good as a circus, but then Kari knew nothing about such a thing as a circus. She watched them with great interest, leaning her long neck over the edge of the cloud in which her nest was built.

Suddenly she saw a sight that made her lean forward so far that she very nearly overbalanced and fell out. Far below her was an open space near a bright spot that she knew was water in a little swampy place in a hollow. The grass there was green and soft; there were trees all round it, and it was a very secluded place, except for anyone looking from above, like the inquisitive Kari.

But Kari was not looking only at green grass and shining water. She saw a little group of birds that had come out of the swamp, where they had been wading, and had begun to dance. They were Native Companions—Puralkas—but Kari did not know that. All she knew was that they were very beautiful creatures, the most beautiful, she thought, that she had ever seen: and they were doing the most interesting things.

Very gracefully they danced to and fro on the patch of green grass. They were tall, slim birds, looking a kind of dim grey colour when seen so far away. Their legs were very long and thin, for they belonged to the tribe of birds called Waders, who get their food by walking in swamps and morasses, and they had neat bodies, not fluffy like some of Kari's own feathers—with which she immediately felt very dissatisfied. Their queer thin heads, with long beaks, were carried on long necks, which twisted about as they danced. They pranced up and down, giving little runs backwards and forwards, marching and stepping in the most curious manner. Never had Kari seen so charming a sight. It made her suddenly envious. Until now, she had regarded all the animals and birds as so much beneath her in every way that it never occurred to her to wish to be like them, or to do anything that they did. But this was the first time that she had seen the Native Companions dance.

Kari's cloud drifted away presently, and she could no longer see the queer grey company of long-legged birds prancing on the green spot in the forest. But nothing that now came within her sight interested her at all. She saw the lyre-birds building their mounds in the Bush, and making them gay with all sorts of odd things: bright stones, bits of quartz, gay feathers; and they also danced on their mounds, but it did not please Kari as much as the dance of the Puralkas. The moon showed her the animals that come out at night—wombat, wallaby, wild dogs, and opossums; native bears climbing up the highest trees, and flying-foxes that trailed like clouds between her and the tree-tops. She saw the

MARY GRANT BRUCE

lizards that live in rocks and on the ground, and the hideous iguanas that run up the trees. Great flocks of screaming cockatoos made the air white, as they flew, the sun gleaming on their yellow crests. There were snakes, too, in the Bush: great carpet-snakes, evil-looking brown and black fellows, and the wicked tiger-snake, with its yellow-patterned back and its quick cruel movements. Once it had amused Kari very much to see the jackass, Merkein, swoop down upon a snake and carry it, struggling, back into a tree. The jackass was a silent bird then, and never made any fuss over his captures: still, it was exciting to see him catch snakes. But now Kari found that none of these things interested or amused her anymore. All she wanted to see again was the Puralkas come out of their swamp and dance upon the grass.

She watched for a long time, hoping always to catch sight of them again; but though her cloud drifted over all kinds of country, she could not find the Puralkas until at last, one day, as she leaned out, to her great joy the little green space came below her again; and there were the long-legged birds, dancing backwards and forwards as they had done before.

She watched them breathlessly, until her cloud began to float away; and then she decided in her mind that she could not bear to let them go again. Indeed, she knew now that unless she could do as they did, she would never feel happy anymore. "I have seen all there is in the world," she said, "and nothing is half so beautiful as dancing. I know I could dance far better than the Puralkas, if I only knew the way. I will go down and get them to teach me how to dance. Then I can fly back to my cloud, and for ever after I shall not need to look at the world, for I shall be too happy dancing on the clouds."

So Kari spread her great wings and floated down the sky until she came over the little green space among the trees. Then she dropped gently, and finally landed in the swamp, which she did not like at all, because she had never before had her feet wet, nor were they made for wading in the soft mud of a swamp. She scrambled out as quickly as she could, folding her wings over her back.

The Puralkas had run back to the edge of their little dancing-ground when they saw the great brown bird coming down from the sky. At first they were inclined to fly away, but they were inquisitive birds, and they waited to see what she would do, though they were quite prepared for flight if she proved to be alarming. But the Emu looked so simple and meek, and she was so comically upset at getting her feet wet, that the Puralkas saw at once that there was no cause for fear. As they were not afraid, they became rather angry, for they did not like strangers to see them dancing. So they clustered together and watched her with unfriendly eyes as she struggled out of the mud and wiped her feet upon the grass.

"How are you?" she said, rather breathlessly. "I have been watching you all from my home in the clouds, and I think you are nice little birds!"

Now, this made the Puralkas exactly seventeen times more angry than before. They believed that they were quite the most beautiful birds that ever wore feathers, and it made them furious to be addressed in this patronizing manner. Who was this awkward brown monster of a bird, to drop out of nowhere and talk to them as if she were a Queen? They chattered among themselves in a whisper.

"She is as ugly as a Jew-lizard," said one.

"Did ever anyone see such great coarse feet?" another whispered. "And her legs!—he-he! Why, they are as thick as the trunk of a tree-fern!"

"And what a great silly head!"

"She is larger than a big rock, but she is more foolish than a coot," said another. "One look at her will tell you that she has no sense."

"And what is that ridiculous thing she said about a home in the clouds?" one asked. "As if we did not know that there is nothing in the clouds except rain!"

"Why, the big Eagle flew up nearly to the sun the other day; and yet he saw nothing of nests in the clouds," said another. "She must think we are very simple, to come to us with such a tale."

"No one could possibly think us simple, unless she were mad," said another. "Everyone knows that we are the wisest birds in all the Bush. She means to insult us!" And they all glared at the Emu, much as if she were a tiger-snake.

Poor Kari felt very puzzled and unhappy. She felt that she had done a kind and condescending thing in coming down to earth and talking so sweetly to these smaller birds; and she could not make out why they should look at her with such angry eyes. She rubbed her muddy feet on the grass, and began to wish that she had never left her nest in the cloud.

"Do you not speak my language?" she asked at last. "Why do you not answer me?"

The Puralkas put their heads together again, and whispered. Finally an old Puralka stepped forward with mincing steps and looked her up and down, so that Kari actually blushed.

"We know what you say, but we do not know why you say it," said the old Puralka. "Why should you want to know how we are? and how dare you call us nice little birds? We do not know what you are—you are something like a bird, to be sure, but in most ways you are a kind of freak. At any rate, we have no love for strangers."

The unfortunate Kari moved her big head from side to side, and looked at the bad-tempered old Puralka in amazement. Her beak opened slowly, but she was too surprised to speak. Nothing like this had ever occurred to her when she lived in the sky.

"As for your extraordinary remark about a home in the clouds, we would like to remind you that we were not hatched yesterday," went on the old Puralka. "Not even the swallows nest in the clouds. You are only wasting your time, and we have none to waste on you. Would you mind going away? We want to get on with our dancing."

Kari did not know what to say. Her bewildered eyes glanced from one Puralka to another, and, finding no friendly face, came back to the old bird who stood waiting for her to answer or go away. She had never dreamed of anything like this, among her drifting clouds, and her first instinct was to spread her wings and fly back until she found her own peaceful nest. But the Puralka's mention of dancing reminded her of what had brought her to earth, and she felt again all the old longing to watch the grey birds dance. So she summoned up her courage, of which she possessed surprisingly little, considering her size.

"I'm sure I don't know why you should be so annoyed," she said meekly. "I mean well, and it grieves me that I have offended you. It was because I thought you *were* nice little birds that I called you so, but of course I do not think so now—that is, I mean, I—" She broke off, for the old Puralka had uttered something like a snort, and was regarding her with a fixed expression of wrath, and all the other Puralkas had bristled alarmingly. "Oh, I don't know what I really *do* mean!" said poor Kari helplessly. "You all look at me so unpleasantly. And it is quite true that I have a nest in the clouds—if you will come up, I will show it to you. I live there always, and I have only come down because I hoped that you would teach me to dance!"

There was silence for a moment, and then all the Puralkas began to laugh. They laughed so much that they could not stand—they went reeling round the little green patch, and at last they sat down, with their legs sticking out straight in front of them, and laughed more and more.

Meanwhile, Kari stood looking at them stupidly. She felt that it was not pleasant laughter.

At last they ceased to laugh, and, putting all their heads together, began to whisper. This went on so long that after a while Kari grew tired of standing, and so she sat down and watched them, feeling very unhappy. Overhead a jackass perched on a big gum-tree, and looked at the group, with his wise old head on one side.

When they had whispered for a long time, the Puralkas got up and stood in a row, with their wings tightly folded over their backs. The old Puralka came forward.

"You must excuse us for laughing," she said. Her voice was not rude now, but there was something in it that made Kari feel as uncomfortable as she had felt when she had been rude before. "We did not mean to hurt your feelings—but we all thought of something funny we saw last month, and so we had to laugh."

If Kari had been less simple, she would have known that this was only said out of politeness, but she was very anxious to make friends, so she looked gratefully at the old Puralka and said, timidly, that she was glad they were so merry.

"Quite so," said the Puralka. "It is a poor heart that never rejoices. But about dancing—that is a different matter. You see, you have wings."

"Eh?" said the Emu stupidly. "Why, of course, I have wings. Why not?"

"Well, that is the difficulty," said the Puralka. "Dancing like ours is the most beautiful thing in the world, of course. But no one with wings can learn it. You see, we have none ourselves."

The Emu gave a quick look at the Puralkas, standing in a row. They had folded their wings so tightly over their neat bodies that it looked as though they had really none at all; and she looked so hard at their bodies that she did not notice how cunning their eyes were.

"Why, I never noticed that yours were gone," she said. "Dear me! how sad! Do you not find it very uncomfortable and awkward?"

"No; why should we?" snapped the Puralka. "Wings are really not much use when you once get accustomed to doing without them. Dancing is much better."

"But why cannot one have both?" asked Kari.

"Simply *because*," said the old Puralka crossly. "We do not know why these things are, and we never ask foolish questions about them. But if you wish to learn our beautiful dancing, you must give up your wings first."

　　　　　　　　　　　　　　　　　　　MARY GRANT BRUCE

"Give up my wings! I could never do that," cried Kari.

"Well, dancing is better. But it is for you to say," said the old Puralka.

As she spoke, she made a sign to the others, and they began to dance, swaying forward until they almost touched Kari, and then backwards again. Then the line broke up into circles and figures, and they danced round the Emu until her head grew dizzy with their movements, and she felt that to dance so well was even better than to have wings. To and fro they went, faster and faster, until she could scarcely distinguish one from another, and their long thin legs she could hardly see at all. Then, quite suddenly, they all stopped; and Kari blinked at them, and could not speak.

"Well?" asked the old Puralka, watching her closely. "Do you not think that wings are only a small price to pay for such dancing?"

"Could you teach me?" Kari asked.

"Easily, if you give up your wings."

Kari gave a great sigh.

"Very well," she said. "I cannot live without knowing how to dance as you do."

"Then, spread your wings out on this stone," said the Puralka.

So Kari spread her great wings across the stone, and the Puralkas cut them off quite close to her body with their sharp beaks.

Then they said,

"Stand up."

Kari stood up, feeling very naked and queer without her wings. Then the Puralkas began to dance again, faster and faster; and they danced upon her wing-feathers that had been cut off, scattering them with their feet until there were not two left together, and the wind came and took the feathers, so that they floated away over the tops of the trees and mounted out of sight. Then the Puralkas laughed again, just as they had laughed before, until Kari's head rang with the noise of it.

"When will you teach me?" she asked timidly.

"Teach you!" cried the Puralkas. "What a joke! What a joke!" They burst out laughing again. Then, to Kari's amazement, they unfolded their wings and shook them in her face. The whole green patch of grass was full of the fluttering of the long grey wings.

"You said you had none!" she cried.

"What a joke! What a joke!" screamed the Puralkas, flapping her with their wings. They spun round and round her, their long legs dancing madly, and their wings quivering and fluttering. Then they suddenly mounted into the air, circled about her once or twice, and flew away through the trees. The sound of their wicked laughter grew fainter and fainter until it died away.

Kari sat down and put her head down on the ground. After a while she got up and tried to fly, but the little stumps of her wings would not raise her an inch from the earth, and very soon she ceased to try. She sat down again.

Later on, she stood up and began to try to dance as the Puralkas had done. She moved her great feet in the same way, and tried to sway about; but it was useless. She looked so comical, hopping round on her thick legs, that the Jackass, which had all the time sat in the gum-tree overhead, broke into a great shout of laughter, and all the Bush rang with the sound. "Ha-ha-ha-ha!—ho-ho-ho-ho!" screamed the Jackass. "Kari is trying to dance—look at her! There never was anything half so funny—ha-ha-ha! ho-ho-ho!"

Then Kari knew that she had lost her wings for nothing; that she could never dance like the Puralkas, and that—worst of all—she could never go back to her nest in the clouds. She could not bear the harsh laughter of the Jackass, and so she ran away, her long legs taking great strides, crashing into the undergrowth of the Bush. Then the Jackass flew away, still chuckling to himself that anyone could be so stupid. Soon the little green patch of grass was quite deserted; until the sun set, when the cruel Puralkas came flying back to it and danced again. But Kari never came to it.

So the Emu lives on earth, and has forgotten all about the nest she once had in the drifting clouds. She has no friends among the birds, for though she is a bird herself, she has no wings, and cannot fly. She has taught herself to run very fast, and to kick with her big feet, so that it is not wise to make her angry. Because she used to live in the clouds and had no proper training, she will eat the most extraordinary things—stones, and nails, and pieces of iron and glass, which the blacks have brought into the Bush—but they never seem to disagree with her. She is not a very happy bird, for all the time she keeps hoping that her wings will grow long again and that she will be able to fly back to find her cloud-nest. But they never grow.

Always since then, Merkein, the Jackass, has been able to laugh. He is called the Laughing Jackass, because of this. He has been a merry fellow ever since he sat on the gum-tree and watched Kari trying to dance, after the cruel Puralkas had robbed her of her wings and left her far away from her nest in the white clouds.

MARY GRANT BRUCE

IV

Booran, the Pelican

Chapter I

Long ago, black people were scattered all over the earth, and the forests and plains were full of them. But a great flood came. For weeks it rained all day and all night, until nearly all the plains were great swamps. Then the snow was washed from the hills, and the rivers and creeks overflowed their banks, and swept over the country. There was scarcely anything to be seen except the tops of the tallest trees sticking out of the waters that covered the land. All the camps were washed away, and nearly all the people were drowned.

In one tribe, the only people left alive were a man and three women. Their camp was near a river; and when the flood came and the river rose and washed away the wurleys, they clung to a great log that lay upon the bank. It was so huge a log that they did not think any flood would ever move it. But they had seen only little floods, and they did not know what the river could do when it rose in its wrath.

The water crept higher and higher as they clung to the log, and at length they felt its great length give a little shiver beneath them. Presently it shifted a little, and the water slipped below it; and soon it swung right round until one end pointed over the bank. Still the flood came rising and rising, and presently a wave flowed right over the log and washed off some of the people who were clinging to it. But the man and the three women dug their fingers into knot-holes and cracks, and held on desperately.

Then a fresh rush of water took the log, and it bumped heavily three times on the bank and slid off into the water. At first, its weight took it under the surface, and the four blacks, feeling the cold dark water close over their heads, made sure that Death had come for them. Still they gripped the log, and presently it rose, and the current whirled it round and sent it off downstream. It bumped heavily on a snag, and one of the women fell off, crying for help as she went. The man leaned over quickly and by good chance gripped her by the hair. Somehow, half pulled, half climbing, she managed to scramble back, and got another grip upon the sodden wood. Then the flood carried them into the darkness.

All through the cold blackness of the night they held to their rocking place of refuge. Sometimes it went aground, with a jar that shook it through its great length, and hung awhile before a fresh spurt of water washed it off again, to float away into the storm-riven night once more. Then there would come bends in the river, when the current would fail to take the log round quickly enough, because it was so long; and it would sail on and ram its nose into the bank, running so far into the soft mud that perhaps an hour would creep past before the washing of the water worked it loose again. Then the log would swing right round, shaking in the eddies, until it seemed that numbed fingers could hold no longer. But still the terrified blacks held on, while their raft spun down the stream once more, with the cold waves splashing over their shivering bodies.

Dawn broke slowly, in the mist of driving rain, and showed them a country covered as far as they could see with water. On either side of the river, the topmost ridge of the high banks still could be seen: but soon these were almost submerged and the log floated in the midst of a great brown sea.

About two hours after sunrise a sudden swirl of water took the log and floated it out upon the top of the left-hand bank. It came to rest with a shock, and one of the women loosened her grip and fell off, with a mournful little cry that she could hold on no more. But to her surprise, the water was only up to her knees, and the log lay at rest beside her, its voyage over.

The man, whose name was Karwin, grunted as he straightened his stiffened limbs, slipping down into the water beside the woman.

"That was good luck for you, Murla," he said. "If the water had been any deeper you would have gone for ever, for there is no strength left in me to pull you out."

"I thought it was the end," said Murla, her teeth chattering with cold. "And, as far as I can see, it might as well have been the end, for it is better to die quickly than slowly, and we shall never get out of this dreary place."

"That is very likely," said Karwin. "But still I am glad to be able to let go of that shaking log and stand upright once more."

The other women had scrambled to a sitting position on the log, and were rubbing their stiffened limbs.

"I think those who stayed in camp will have died more comfortably than we shall," said one. "How are we to get any food?"

"Oh, there will be no food," Karwin answered. "Unless the flood goes down very quickly, we shall certainly starve. I do not even know where we are, and I have no weapons. Ky! none of our forefathers ever knew such a flood! It is something to have seen it!"

"That will not do us much good when we are lying dead in the mud," said Murla shortly. "I would rather have a piece of kangaroo now than see the biggest flood that ever was in the world. I have had enough of floods! Do you think the water will come any higher?"

"How can I tell?" answered Karwin shortly. Then, because they were all tired, and frozen, and hungry, they quarrelled about it, and became almost warm in the discussion. After awhile, Karwin laughed.

"If I had a waddy I would give all three of you something to argue over," he said. "What is the use of becoming angry when there is nothing to be gained by it? It will not take us off this bank, that is certain."

"No, but it keeps us from thinking," Murla said. "When I was angry just now I quite forgot that I was hungry."

"All women are a little mad," said Karwin scornfully. "No amount of talking could ever make me forget that I was hungry. It is the most important thing in the world."

He looked about him. Behind the ridge of the river bank, on which their log lay, the current of the flooded stream swept by, deep and swift. Before, the sea of brown water stretched as far as he could see, broken only by clusters of storm-washed leaves, that were the tops of submerged trees. There, no current ran; but the wind fled along the surface of the water and blew it into ripples and little waves.

"I wonder how deep that is," said Karwin thoughtfully. "I will go and see."

He took a few careful steps forward. Then his foot slipped, and he slid off the mud of the crest of the bank, and immediately disappeared with a loud splash. The women set up a dreadful screaming, crying "Come back!"—which, under the circumstances, was a very stupid thing to say. For a long moment the world seemed empty before them.

Then Karwin's head suddenly popped up out of the water, with his face very wet and angry. He swam to the ridge, but it was not easy to get upon it, for the crest was sharp, and very slippery, as Karwin already knew to his cost. Several times he clawed at it, only to slide back into the deep water, spluttering and wrathful.

"Hold on to the log," said Murla, quickly, to one of the women. "Then give your sister your other hand, and she can hold mine."

The three formed a chain and found that, by stretching as far as they could reach, Murla could just touch Karwin with her hand. He made a great effort and caught it in a firm grip, and then they pulled all together, and so managed to tug him over the edge of the ridge.

Karwin was very angry, and not at all grateful to them.

"You might have thought of that sooner," he growled. "Ky! the water is cold, and I sank down into a clump of prickly bushes, so that I am stuck with prickles all over. There is no getting away from this bank, that is certain."

"We had suspected that," said Murla, laughing. At this Karwin became worse-tempered than ever, for a blackfellow does not like to be laughed at by a woman, anymore than a white man likes it. He threatened to beat them all, and even struck out at one of the women who was grinning, but Murla spoke to him severely.

"Don't do that!" she said boldly. "We are all in the same fix together, and we will not be beaten by you. If you strike one of us we will all push you off into the deep water—and this time we will not pull you back. Therefore, you had better be warned."

Murla looked so fierce as she spoke that Karwin stopped the hand he was lifting to strike the woman, and scratched his head with it instead. It was quite a new experience for a blackfellow to be ordered about by a lubra, and you can fancy that he did not like it. Still, the other women were clearly prepared to back up Murla; and he did not forget how he had struggled in the water at the edge of the bank before they pulled him in. So, instead of hitting the woman, he growled unpleasantly and waded to one end of the log, where he sat down and gave himself up to very bad temper. This time, however, he kept it inside him, and so it did not hurt anyone.

The sisters looked at Murla with great respect, but Murla only laughed at them. She was a pretty woman, for a lubra. Her hair was long and very black and curly, and she was much fairer than most of her tribe, with a fine flat nose and a merry smile. None of her teeth had been knocked out, which happens to many lubras, and so there were no holes in her smile. She was little more than a girl, but she was tall and strong, and very clever. And she was not at all afraid of Karwin.

For two days the four castaways sat on their log and watched the flood. Once it rose higher, when a fresh mass of snow was washed

MARY GRANT BRUCE

from the distant hill-tops, and came down to swell the river; and they thought their log was again about to be carried down-stream, and gave themselves up for lost, for they knew that now they were too weak to hold on for very long. But the log held firm upon the bank, and the danger passed. It was very cold. They plastered themselves all over with a thick coating of mud, hoping that when it dried it would keep them warmer; and this helped against the cold wind, though it was not at all comfortable in other ways.

But worst of all was hunger. On the second day they began to break pieces off the log and chew them, and that, as you can imagine, did very little good. Karwin became more and more bad-tempered, and looked at the women as if it was their fault. Also, he was very sore from the prickles, and the two sisters and Murla spent quite a long time in picking them out of his back, though he was only a little grateful to them.

On the second day, the water began to go down. The river still roared and raced past them, bearing on its breast all kinds of things: trees, logs, bushes, interlaced fragments of ruined wurleys, drowned animals, and even dead blacks; but its water slipped back from the bank where their log lay, until it left them on a little mud island, with the brown sea still rippling about them in every direction. The tops of the trees came farther and farther out of the water, and new tree-tops came into view, with their boughs laden with mud. Often they saw little living animals in the brushwood that went drifting by them in the river; and nearly all the floating rubbish was alive with snakes that had taken refuge from the flood. Sometimes the brushwood would break up in the current, and they would see the snakes swimming wildly until the river carried them out of sight. Two came ashore on their island, and Karwin killed them with a stick he had taken out of the river. They ate them, and felt a little better. But they knew that they must soon die if they did not get more food. They watched the river anxiously, hoping that it might bring them something else.

Towards evening, they were gazing up-stream, when Murla cried out suddenly.

"What is that?" she said, pointing to a dark spot on the water.

"It is a bush," said one of the women, in a dull voice.

"No, I am certain it is an animal," Murla said. "It is floating towards us. Let us try to get it."

So they held hands, as they had done when Karwin fell in, and Karwin slipped into the current, holding Murla's hand tightly. He had found a stick with a sharp hook on one end, where a branch had broken off, and when the dark object came bobbing down-stream he thrust at it fiercely, savage with hunger. The hook caught in it, and very carefully they drew it ashore, and managed to get it on their island. It was a harder matter to get Karwin back, but they managed that too, and then they all lay on the mud and panted, and, except for Murla's fair face, they looked as if they were part of the mud.

Their find was a plump young wombat, and it probably saved their lives. Of course they had no way of cooking it, but at the moment that scarcely troubled them; neither did they at all object to the fact that it had been dead for a good while. They ate it all, and long after the moon had come out to cast her white light into the flood it showed them sitting on the log, happily crunching the bones.

Chapter II

BOORAN WAS A VERY CLEVER bird. He was bigger than most of the water-fowl, and very strong. He was also very proud, partly because of his great wings, which would carry his heavy body skimming over the lakes and swamps, and partly because of his beautiful white plumage. All his feathers were perfectly white, and he was so vain about it that he scorned every bird that had coloured or dark plumage. He used to look at his reflection in deep pools, and murmur, "How beautiful I am!" If by any mischance he got a mud-stain on his feathers he was quite unhappy until he had managed to wash it off. Some people might not think a pelican a very lovely bird, but Booran was completely satisfied with himself.

Besides being beautiful and white, Booran at that time owned a bark canoe. It made him prouder than ever. It was not a very big canoe, but it was as much as a pelican could comfortably manage. He used to sit in it and paddle it along with his strong wings. There was really no reason why he should have had a canoe at all, for he was quite able to swim about in the water with far less labour than it needed to paddle his boat with his wings. It was only part of his great pride.

Still, no other bird had ever thought of having a canoe, so it pleased Booran to think himself superior to them all. No other bird wanted one at all, but he forgot that. The Emu laughed at him openly, and when Booran offered him a trip in his canoe he asked rudely what Booran thought he could do with his long legs in such a cockle shell? That made Booran more indignant than he had ever been since two black swans had risen suddenly under the canoe one day and upset both it and Booran in a very muddy part of a lake. He vowed that no other bird should ever enter it. Sometimes a meek little bird, such as a honey-eater or a bell-bird, would perch on the edge of the canoe and ask to be ferried about; but Booran never would allow it. He used to catch fish, and when he had stored all he could in his pouch he would put the rest in the canoe, so that soon it became all one dreadful smell. Not that any people in the country of the blacks were likely to object to that. They were brought up on smells.

When the big flood came, Booran enjoyed himself thoroughly. The river was too swift for him to attempt in his canoe at first, but he paddled about in the water that covered the plains, and poked into a great many things that did not concern him in the least. Sometimes he ran aground, when it was always an easy matter for him to jump overboard and push the canoe off with his great beak. He found all kinds of new things to eat, floating round in the flood-water; and some of them gave him indigestion rather badly. But on the whole it was a very interesting time, and he was very glad that he had a canoe so that he could go about in a stylish manner.

It was on the afternoon of the third day after the water had begun to go down, that Booran was first able to try the canoe on the river. The current was still swift, but he kept in the quieter water near each bank, and did not find much difficulty in getting about. He saw a number of strange blacks on a rise near the water, busily building wurleys; but they did not see him, for he dodged under cover of the wattle-trees fringing the bank. Then he pulled down-stream for a little while, until he came to where the banks were lower, and not many trees were to be seen out of the water. He rounded a bend, and came upon Karwin and his companions.

Booran's first instinct was to get out of sight. He was afraid of all blackfellows, especially when they had spears and throwing-sticks. But before he could go, the woman Murla saw him, and uttered a great cry of astonishment. At once they believed that it was Magic—so many strange things could be explained that way. They watched the big white bird in his bark canoe, and waited to see what would happen, hoping that he was not an evil spirit who would do them any harm.

Seeing them so quiet, and realizing that they were unarmed, Booran allowed his natural curiosity to get the better of him. He paddled across the river, swept down a little by the current, and stopped his canoe in a quiet pool near the mud island, where the castaways sat miserably on their log. They looked so forlorn and unhappy that even his cold and fishy heart was stirred.

"Good day," he said.

"Good day," Karwin answered.

"This is a big flood," Booran remarked.

"Yes, it is a very big one. All the land has gone away."

"Yes, but it will come back. Fish are scarce, now that the river is high."

"That is very likely," said Karwin.

Then, having made all these stupid remarks, as all men do before they come to business, they stopped, and looked at the sky, and Booran said, "I wonder if more rain will come!"

Murla struck in suddenly.

"Men are very strange," she said. "They are always ready to jabber. How is it that you go about in that little boat?"

"Because I like it," said Booran shortly, for he did not approve of women talking so freely, neither did he like the question about his canoe.

Murla laughed. "You look very funny when you are cross," she said. "I never saw such a dignified pelican." The other women shuddered, for they thought that Booran might be an evil spirit, in which case he would certainly object to such free-and-easy remarks. But Booran looked at Murla, and saw how pretty she was, and suddenly he did not wish to be angry. Instead, he smiled at her; and no one who has not seen it can imagine how peculiar a pelican looks when he smiles.

"It is a very useful canoe," he said. "I have been all over the flood-waters in it, and have seen many wonderful things."

"Have you any food?" asked Murla eagerly.

"No, for I have eaten it all. But I may come across some at anytime. Would you like it?"

"Like it!" said Murla. "Why, we have only had two snakes and a wombat between us for four days—and the wombat was only a little one. I could eat the quills of a porcupine!"

"Dear me," said Booran, looking at her with his foolish little eyes very wide. "That would be very unpleasant, would it not? I quite regret that I ate an old fish that I found in the stern of my canoe this morning. Not that it would have made much of a meal for four people."

"It would have given me a breakfast," said Karwin rudely. "But as there is no food, there is no use in talking about it. Tell me, Pelican, have you seen any of our people? We do not know if there are any left alive."

"I have seen some blacks, but I do not know if they are your people," Booran answered. "They are across the river, where they are building themselves new huts."

"Can't you go and see if they belong to our tribe?"

Booran shook his big head decidedly.

"Not I," he said. "Most blacks are very uncivil to pelicans, and these had weapons close at hand. I have no wish to be found with a spear sticking in my heart, or in any other part of me."

"Did you notice what they were like?" Murla asked eagerly.

"I saw a fat woman, and a thin man," said Booran stupidly. "How should I know what they were like? They are not beautiful like pelicans. Oh, and I saw a very tall man, with a red bone through his nose. He was sitting idly on a stump while the others worked."

"That was my husband!" said Murla with a faint shriek. "Alas, I thought he was drowned! And the fat woman may be your wife, Goomah," she said to Karwin.

"Very likely," said Karwin. "Did you notice if they had food?"

"I do not know. But it is likely, for they had fire, and there was a pleasant smell."

"If my wife Goomah has food and fire, while I have nothing, there will be trouble," said Karwin wrathfully.

"That may be, but we will die here without ever knowing," Murla said. "Long before the water goes down we will have starved to death, and then nothing will matter." She broke off a bit of wood and flung it into the swirling river. "I wish we had never tried to save ourselves, or seen that hateful log!"

Now, Booran had been watching Murla, and he thought she looked very capable, and he thought that she could be very useful to him if he could get her away to some place where she could catch fish for him, so that he might spend all his time admiring himself and paddling about in his canoe.

But he did not quite know how to manage it.

Karwin and the woman went on wrangling. They had not been happy before Booran came with his tidings; but now they could only think of their fellow-blacks feasting and making a warm and comfortable camp, and it made them feel very much worse than they had felt before. They shouted long and loudly in the hope of making the others hear; but no answer came, and the river rushed by them without pity, and they hated their little mud island.

All the time, Booran gazed at Murla, and at last he made up his mind that he could not possibly do without her. Whatever happened, he must get her away, and sail with her in his bark canoe to an island where the blacks could never find her. The others were talking so fast that he had time to think out a plan, and when they stopped for lack of breath, he spoke.

"I think, if you sat very still and got in and out very carefully, that I could take you across the river, one at a time," he said, speaking in a great hurry.

"That thing would sink," said Karwin sulkily, looking at the little canoe with eyes of scorn.

"No, it does not sink easily. You would have to be very careful, but it would be safe."

Karwin looked at the canoe, and then he looked at the trees that showed round the bend, when the high banks were quite clear of water. It was very tempting to think of getting there—such a little way! He thought hard. Then he said:

"You can take Kari first—she is the lightest, and if the canoe does not sink with her, perhaps I will go."

Booran did not care which he took first, so long as it was not Murla. But the woman Kari objected very strongly, and made a great outcry, for she thought she would be drowned. However, the others were all agreed that she should go, so there was no use in objecting, and she had to give in. Crying and trembling, she stepped into the canoe, which Booran brought close to the bank.

The canoe went down a good deal, but it did not sink, and Booran paddled gently up the stream, keeping very close to the bank, so that the current did not sweep him down. He disappeared round the bend, and for awhile Karwin and the two women who were left watched anxiously, fearing to see the upturned canoe float back empty. But in about ten minutes they saw Booran turn the corner and paddle swiftly down, evidently very pleased with himself. When he got near the mud island he called out, "All is well! I landed her easily on the bank, and she has run to the camp."

That made the others eager, and Murla stepped forward to get into the canoe. But Booran stopped her, saying, "Not now—next time!"—and before she could argue, Karwin twisted her out of his way, and stepped into the canoe so hurriedly that it nearly sank, and Booran called out very angrily to him to mind what he was doing. However, the canoe righted itself, and presently Booran had paddled it out of sight again.

Murla began to feel a little uneasy, though she scarcely knew why. There was something wrong about the way that Booran looked at her, with his cold eyes that were so like a fish's. She felt she would be glad when she was out of his canoe, and safely on the same side as her people. She did not want to get into the canoe at all; but as it was necessary to do so, she decided to get it over as soon as possible. So she said to the other black woman, "I will go next, Meri."

"All right," said Meri, shivering under her little 'possum rug and her coat of mud. "But tell the Pelican to hurry back, or I shall certainly die of cold."

Murla waited impatiently until Booran appeared, and when the canoe came alongside the bank she was ready. But Booran looked at her queerly, and said, "Not now—next time!

"Why?" asked Murla angrily. "This is my turn."

"Not now—next time!" was all Booran would say; and he beckoned to Meri, who was not slow to obey, for she was very tired of waiting. She stepped in, and the canoe moved away from the mud island.

Suddenly Murla was very much afraid, although as a rule she did not know what fear meant. She felt that she must not get into Booran's canoe—that there was danger coming very close to her. In a few minutes he would be back for her. A quick resolve came to her mind. Whatever happened, Booran must not find her there when he came back.

She slipped off her 'possum rug and wrapped it round a log that had come ashore on their island. It was just as long as she was, and when the rug was wrapped about it, it looked as if she were lying asleep. Then she slipped into the river, and began to swim across.

Booran and Meri were out of sight round the bend, and what she wanted to do was to get to the other side before the canoe came back. But it was not an easy matter. The current was swift, and though she was a very strong swimmer, it took her down-stream; and once she thought that she must be drowned. However, just as she was on the point of giving up, she felt the ground under her feet, and scrambled out upon a bank that was nearly all under water. Then she waded along it until she got near the bend.

Just then she heard the noise of Booran's wings brushing in the water. She flung herself down on her face—just in time, for the canoe came round the bend, and passed quite close to her. Booran heard the swirl in the water, and glanced round, seeing the ripples; but just then he caught sight of what looked like Murla, lying on the mud island, and he said, "Oh, it was only a water rat!" and paddled on.

Murla lay still in the water, holding her breath, until he had floated down the stream. Then she got up very quietly and waded, sinking in the soft mud of the bank until it grew higher, and trees and dry land could be seen. She ran then, casting her eyes wildly about until she saw ahead a little drift of smoke; and presently, toiling up a steep rise in the bank, she came upon the blacks, where already Karwin and Meri and Kari were jabbering loudly, telling all their experiences and hearing those of the others at the same time. They cried out with astonishment when they saw Murla coming along the bank, and asked her why Booran had not brought her in his canoe.

When she told them she had been afraid of him, they all laughed at her. But her husband, the tall man with the red bone through his nose, was very angry because she had left her 'possum rug behind, and asked her if she thought rugs like that grew on wild cherry-trees. He went off at once to see if he could get it back, telling her as he went that if he failed, she need not think she was going to have his. Of course, Murla had known that already.

Meanwhile, Booran had paddled down to the mud island, and, seeing the form in the 'possum rug, lying under the shelter of the great log, he called to it several times, saying, "Come on, now. It is your turn." But no movement came, and at last he grew angry, and hopped out of the canoe and went on to the island, still calling. There was no answer, and he lost his temper and kicked the figure very hard—with the result that he hurt his foot very much. Then he pulled the rug off roughly, and found only a log underneath.

Booran became furious. He had been made to look a fool. For awhile he stamped about the island, screaming in his rage, and when the blacks got to the opposite bank that is how they saw him. Then Booran made up his mind that he would "look out fight," as the blacks do, and kill the husband of the woman.

So he took some mud and smeared it on himself in long lines, so that he might be striped as the blacks are when they go fighting: for a blackfellow does not consider himself dressed for battle until he has painted himself in long white streaks with pipeclay. He was so busy painting, and planning how he would slay Murla's husband, that he did not see a black shadow in the sky. It was another pelican, and he came nearer, puzzled to know what could be this strange thing, so like a pelican and yet striped like a fighting man. He could not make it out, but he decided it could not be right; and so he drove at Booran and struck him in the throat with his great beak, killing him. Then he flew away.

Now the blacks say, there are no black pelicans anymore. They are all black and white, just as Booran was when his Death came to him suddenly out of the sky.

The blacks across the river were very much amazed. But when the great black Pelican had sailed away, Murla's husband swam across and got her 'possum rug, which he brought back, tied on top of his head. He gave it back to Murla, and then beat her with his waddy for having been so careless as to leave it behind. So they lived happily ever after.

But the river took Booran's little canoe and whisked it away. It bobbed upon the brown water like a walnut shell, spinning in the eddies, and sailing proudly where the water was clear and free. At each mile the river grew wider and fuller, and the little canoe sped onwards on its breast. Then ahead came a long line of gleaming silver, and the river sang that it had nearly reached the sea. The light canoe rocked over the waters of the bar, but came safely through them; and then it floated away westward, into the sunset.

But the tide brought it back to shore, and the breakers took it and flung it on the rocks, pounding it on their sharp edges until it was no longer a canoe, but only a twisted bit of bark. The waves went back and left it lying on the beach; and some blacks who came along, hungry and cold, were very glad to find it and use it to start their fire, when it was dry. So Booran's canoe was useful to the blacks until the very end.

V

The Story of the Stars

Pund-jel, who was Maker of Men, sat in his high place one day and looked at the world. The blacks believed that in the very long ago he had made the first men and women out of clay; and from there they had spread over all the earth. Pund-jel had made them to be good and happy, and for a long while he had been satisfied with them. But now it was different, and he was angry.

All over the world he could see his black people. They had grown tall and strong, and he thought them beautiful. They were skilled in hunting, and fierce in battle: the women were clever at making rugs of skins, at cooking, at weaving curious mats and baskets of pliant rushes. The forests were full of game for them—birds, beasts and reptiles, all good to eat: there were fish in the lakes and rivers, fat mud-eels in the creeks and swamps, and gum and manna to be found on every hill-side. The world was a good, green world, and there should have been only happiness. But the people themselves had grown wicked.

Pund-jel bent his brows with anger as he looked down upon them. Instead of being peaceful and content, his people had grown fierce and savage. They thought only of fighting and conquest, and were too lazy to work. The laws that he had made for them were as naught in their eyes. They said, "Oh, Pund-jel is very far away. He will never come down into our world to see what we do. Why should we obey him?" So they did just as they pleased, and all the world was evil because of their wickedness.

Pund-jel thought gravely as he looked down into his world, and all the sky was dark with the blackness of his frown.

"My people have grown too many," he said. "When they were few, each helped the other: there was no time for feuds or fighting, for all had to work together in order to live. Now all is changed. They are many and powerful, and they over-run the world, and each man hates his brother. It were better if I made them fewer, and scattered them far and wide. I will send my whirlwinds upon the earth."

So Pund-jel caused storms and fierce winds to arise often, and they swept across the world. In the flat lands there came suddenly whirlwinds of great force, that twisted and eddied through the plains, carrying men aloft in their choking embrace, and letting them fall, broken and dead, miles away from the places where they had lived. On the mountains great hurricanes blew shrieking from peak to peak, tearing up the largest trees by their roots, and tossing them down into the fern-strewn gullies far below. Huge boulders were loosened and went crashing down; and often a landslip followed them, when all the soil would be stripped from a hill-side and fall, thundering, carrying with it hundreds of people and leaving the bare rock behind it, like a scar upon the side of the mountain. Thunder and lightning came and shook the world with terror: mighty trees were riven and shattered, and fires swept through forest and plain, leaving blackness and desolation behind. Then came floods, that covered the low-lying parts of the earth, and made of the rivers roaring torrents, that ran madly to the sea. The world trembled in the terror of the wrath of Pund-jel.

And yet, men had grown so wise and cunning that not very many died. When the whirlwinds and hurricanes came, they crept into holes in the hill-sides, or sheltered themselves in deep gullies. They strengthened their houses, so that the wind should not blow them away. Sometimes they floated down the rivers in bark canoes; and a great number found refuge in caves. Those who were killed were the careless ones, who would not take the trouble to protect themselves against the fury of the storms, thinking that they would only be ordinary gales; but though they died, innumerable people were left.

Just for a little while, they were afraid. They knew they were wicked, and that Pund-jel must be angry with them; and the thought that possibly the storms were the message of his wrath made them careful for awhile. But as time passed they forgot the storms and whirlwinds, and the fate of their brothers and sisters who had been killed; and they went back to their wickedness, becoming worse than they had been before.

And then there came a day when Pund-jel's anger broke anew.

One morning a blackness came out of the sky, and in the blackness a flame of gleaming fire. The people clustered together, in terror, and there were cries of "Pund-jel! Pund-jel is coming!" Then the magic-men began to chatter and make Magic, hoping to turn the wrath of the Maker of Men; and the people flung themselves upon the ground, crying aloud, and calling upon the good Spirits to save them.

The blackness swooped down upon the earth. In the air were strange whisperings and mutterings, as if even the rustling leaves and the boughs of the trees were crying, "Pund-jel is coming!" And then, out of the glowing heart of the cloud came Pund-jel himself, that he might see these men and women that he had made. He spoke no word. His glance was like lightnings, playing about the stricken eyes of those that gazed. But he trod among the black multitudes, and the noise of the trampling of his feet shook the earth.

In his hand he carried his great stone knife, and the sight of it was very terrible. Those who looked upon it fell back blindly. But as he walked on he cut his way among the people, with great sweeps of the cruel weapon, sparing none that came in his way, and cutting them into small fragments. And then the blackness of the cloud received him again, and hid him from the people of the world.

But the pieces of the slain were not dead. Each fragment moved, as Tur-ror, the worm, moves; and from them rose a cry. It came from the fragments of those who had been good men and good women, yet who had met Death at the knife of Pund-jel with the guilty ones.

Then a great and terrible storm came out of the sky, sweeping over the places where Pund-jel had trod; and with it a whirlwind, that gathered up the pieces of those who had been men, women and children, and they became like flakes of snow, white and whirling in the blackness of the air. They were carried away into the clouds.

And when they came to where Pund-jel sat, once more looking down upon the world, he took the flakes that had been bad men and women, and with his hand scattered them so far over the earth that no man could say where they fell. So they passed for ever from the sight of man, and now they lie in the waste places of the world, where there is neither light nor day.

But Pund-jel took the snowflakes that had been good men and women, and he made them into stars. Right up into the blue sky he flung them; and the sky caught them and held them fast, and the light of the sun fell upon them so that they caught some of his brightness. There they stay for ever, and you would not know that they are in any way different from the other stars that twinkle at you on a frosty night when the sky is all blue and silver. Only the magic-men, who know everything, can tell you which among the stars were once good men, women and children, before Pund-jel left his high seat to punish the wickedness of the world.

VI

How Light Came

The blacks believed that the earth was quite flat, with the sky arched above it. They had an idea that if anyone could get beyond the edge of the sky he would come to another country, with rivers and trees, where live the ghosts of all the people who have died. Some thought that there was water all round the edge of the earth. They were taught that at first the sky had lain flat on the ground, so that neither sun, moon, nor stars could move, but the magpies came along and propped it up with long sticks, resting some parts on the mountains near the edge. And sometimes word was sent from tribe to tribe, saying that the props were growing rotten, and unless the people sent up tomahawks to cut new props, the sky would fall. In its falling it would burst, and all the people would be drowned. This used to alarm the blacks greatly, and they would make the magic-men weave charms so that the sky should not fall.

At first, all the earth was in darkness; and at that time there lived among the blacks a man called Dityi. In his tribe was a very beautiful woman whose name was Mitjen; and she became Dityi's wife.

At first Dityi and Mitjen were very happy. They had plenty to eat, and the camp was warm and comfortable, and they loved each other very much. There were no white men, at that time: the blacks ruled all their country, which they thought was the whole world. The forests were full of game, and the rivers of fish: everyone had enough, so there was no fighting. And Dityi thought he was the luckiest man in the world, because he had won the love of Mitjen.

But a stranger came to the camp: a tall dark-eyed man named Bunjil. He told stories of far-away forests and wonderful things to be found there. The other blacks used to listen to him, greatly interested; and no one listened more attentively than Mitjen, for she had a great longing to see the wonderful places of which Bunjil spoke. When she heard him tell stories of these strange lands of the Bush, she burned to leave her quiet home and go exploring. Dityi could not understand this feeling at all. It interested him to hear Bunjil's tales, but he had no wish to do more than hear them. He was very well satisfied with his life, and thought that his own home was better than any other place could possibly be.

But Bunjil soon noticed the dark-eyed girl who never lost a word of his stories. It amused him to see her face light up and her eyes sparkle at his talk; and so he told more and more stories, and did not always trouble to make them true, so long as he could make Mitjen look interested. Sometimes he would meet her wandering alone outside the camp, and then he would tell her, as if he were sorry for her, that this quiet camp was no place for her at all. "You are so beautiful," he would say, "that you should be far away in my wonderful country, where you would see many great men and lovely women; but none more lovely than Mitjen. In this dull hole you are buried alive."

None of this was true, but Bunjil spoke exactly as if it were, and after a time Mitjen began to be very discontented. The simple happy life in the Bush pleased her no longer; she only wanted the exciting things of which Bunjil told. At home, everybody was good to her and liked her, but she was only a girl who had to obey other people all the time, and no one but Dityi had ever troubled about telling her that she was beautiful. Moreover, she could see that Bunjil did not think much of Dityi. He called him one day to Mitjen, "an ignorant black fellow," and though Mitjen could not imagine any people who were not black, it sounded very uncomplimentary, and she could not forget it. As soon as he had said it, Bunjil apologized, saying that it was only a slip of the tongue—but in her heart Mitjen knew this was not true. It made her look down on Dityi a little, and wonder if he were really worthy of her.

One day she asked him if he would take her to Bunjil's country, and his surprise prevented him from speaking for some time. He could only look at her, with his mouth open.

"Go away from home!" he said at last. "Why? What is there to go for?"

"To see the world," said Mitjen, tossing her head. "I do not want to stay for ever in this weary place."

"But it is the world—or most of it," returned Dityi. "I do not know where Bunjil's country is—but the men there cannot be up to much if they are like him, for he is more useless than anyone I ever saw. He cannot throw a boomerang better than a girl, and with a spear I could beat him with my left hand!"

"You are boastful," said Mitjen coldly. "Throwing weapons is not everything."

"Well, I don't know how things are managed in Bunjil's country, but it is very important in ours that a man should know how to throw," said Dityi. "Perhaps Bunjil's game comes close to him to be killed, but here a man has to hunt it. Did Bunjil mention if it came ready cooked too? I don't suppose you would want to do any work in that country of his!"

This made Mitjen very angry, and she quarrelled fiercely with Dityi for making fun of her; and then Dityi lost his temper and beat her a little, which was quite a usual thing to happen to a woman among the blacks. But Mitjen had been told by Bunjil that in his country a man never raised his hand against a woman. So it made her furious to be beaten by Dityi, though he cared for her too much really to hurt her, and she broke away from him and ran to the camp, sobbing that she hated him and did not want to see him anymore.

Near the camp she met Bunjil, who asked her why she was crying; and when she told him, he was kind to her, patting her gently, and pretending to be very angry with Dityi. He was safe in doing this, for Dityi had gone off whistling into the Bush—not sorry that he had beaten Mitjen, if it should make her sensible again, but sorry that she was unhappy, and resolved to bring her back a snake or something equally nice for supper. So Bunjil ran no risk in abusing him, and he did it heartily. When they had finished talking, Mitjen walked away from him into the camp with a very determined face. She went straight to her wurley, and though Dityi brought her home a beautiful young snake and a lace-lizard, she would eat nothing and refused to come out of the wurley to speak to him. So Dityi went back to the young men's huts, angry and offended, and Mitjen lay down, turning her face to the wall. She was just as determined; but only her own heart knew how much she was afraid.

When the people of the camp awoke, she was gone. Nowhere was there any trace of her. And when the blacks went to look for Bunjil, in his wurley, he was gone, too. Then they fell into a great rage, and the young men painted themselves in white stripes with pipeclay, and went forth in pursuit, carrying all their arms, and led by Dityi. But though they looked for many days, they could never come upon a track; and so at last the other young men gave up the search, and went back to the camp. But Dityi did not go back. There was nothing for him at home now that he had lost Mitjen; and so he went on, hunting through the dark forests for his lost love.

Bunjil and Mitjen had fled far into the Bush. For a long time they walked in the creek, so that they would leave no tracks, and if they came to deep holes, they swam them. They were far away from Mitjen's country before they dared to leave the water, and already the girl was tired. But Bunjil would not let her stop to rest, for he knew that they would be pursued. He hurried her on, forgetting now to be gentle when he spoke to her.

It was not many days before Mitjen realized the terrible mistake she had made. They fled deeper and deeper into the Bush, but no wonderful country came in sight. She was often cold and hungry, and Bunjil made her work harder than she had ever worked before, doing not only the woman's work, but a large share of the man's. She found out that he was almost too lazy to get food, and if she had not hunted for game herself, she would never have had enough to eat. Bunjil had told her that he loved her, but very soon she knew that this was not true, and that all he had wanted was a woman to cook for him and help him procure food.

At first she used to ask him when they would come to his own country, and he would put her off, saying, "Presently—pretty soon." But before long she found that it made him angry to be asked about it; and at last, if she spoke of it, he beat her cruelly. So Mitjen did not ask anymore.

Then all the memories of Dityi and his love came crowding upon her, and her heart quite broke. She did not want to live anymore. She lay down under a big log, and when Bunjil spoke to her there was no answer. So he kicked her, and left her. But after he had slept, he went to see why she lay so still; and he found that she was dead.

As he looked at her, a great storm came out of the Bush and whirled him away. It flung him far up in the sky, where you may see him now, if you look closely: a lonely, wandering star, finding no rest anywhere, and no mate. Always he must wander on and on, and never stop, no matter how tired he may be; and the other stars shrink from him, hurrying away if they cross his path.

The storm took Mitjen also, and carried her gently into the sky; and there she saw Dityi, who lit it all up, for he had been turned into the Sun, and was giving light to the earth. But always, the blacks say, he is seeking Mitjen. Like a great fire, he leaps through the sky, mourning for his love and going back and forth in ceaseless quest of her. His wurley is in Nganat, just over the edge of the earth; and the bright colour of sunset is caused by the spirits of the dead going in and out of

Nganat, while Dityi looks among them for his lost love. But he never finds her; and so next day he begins to hunt again, and goes tramping across the sky. Sometimes he shouts her name—"Mitjen! Mitjen!"—and it is then that we hear Thunder go rolling round the world. But Mitjen never answers.

She has been made the Moon, and always she mourns far away and alone. When she sees the glory of the Sun, and hears his trampling feet, she hides herself, for now she is ashamed to let him find her. She only comes from her hiding-place when he sleeps; and then she hurries through the sky, so that she may have the comfort of going in his footsteps, though she knows now that she can never hope to overtake him. Sometimes she sighs, and then a soft breeze flutters over the earth; and the big rain is the tears that relieve her grief.

VII

The Frog that Laughed

Before Pund-jel, Maker of Men, peopled the earth with the black tribes, and very long before the first white man came to Australia, the animals which inhabited the land fell into a great trouble. And this is how it happened. Old Conara, the black chief, told it to me while we were fishing for cod in the Murray one hot night; and he had it from his father, whose mother had told him about it; while to her the story had come from her grandfather, who said he was a little boy when his grandfather had told him, saying he had had the story from Conara, the magpie, after whom he was named. And the magpies learn everything, so you see he ought to know.

Conara said that once in the long-ago time, all the animals were living very cheerfully together, when suddenly all the water disappeared. They went to sleep with the creeks and swamps full, and the rivers running; and when they woke up, everything was dry. Of course, this was the most terrible thing that could happen to the animals, for though they can manage with very little food in Australia, at a pinch, they must always have plenty of water. They searched everywhere for it, through the scrub and over the plains; and the birds flew great distances, always seeking with their eyes for a gleam of water. But it had quite gone.

So the animals held a council of war, and Mirran, the Kangaroo, spoke to them. At a council, some one must always speak first, to tell those present what they know already; and Mirran did this very thoroughly, so that little Kur-bo-roo, the Native Bear, went to sleep and began to climb up the legs of the Emu in his sleep, thinking she was a tree. This led to a disturbance, and it was some time before Mirran could go on again with his speech. Then he found he had forgotten the rest of what he meant to say, so he contented himself by asking them all what they meant to do about it, and remarking that the matter was now open for discussion. This is a remark often made at meetings.

Then Mirran sat down thankfully, but in his relief at finishing his speech he sat on Kowern, the Porcupine; and Kowern is the most uncomfortable seat in the Bush. Mirran got up more quickly than he

MARY GRANT BRUCE

had sat down, and again there was disorder in the meeting, especially as the Jackass was unfeeling enough to laugh.

When matters were more quiet, Kellelek, the Cockatoo, made a long speech, but it was hard to understand what he said, because all his brothers would persist in speaking at the same time. Everyone knew that he wanted water, but as everyone was in the same fix, it did not seem to help along matters to have him say so. Booran, the Pelican, was even more troubled about it than Kellelek, for of course he lived on the water, and he wanted fish badly. All the fish had disappeared, and the eels had buried themselves deep in the soft mud of the beds of the rivers and creeks, and none of the water-fowl had any food. The Red Wallaby, Waat, and old Warreen, the bad-tempered Wombat, made speeches, and so did Meri, the black Dingo, and Tonga, the 'Possum, and a great many other animals. But not one could suggest any means of getting water back, or form an idea as to how it had gone away.

They were all talking together, getting rather hot and excited, and very thirsty, when they heard a sudden whirr of wings overhead, and a bird came dropping down into their midst. It was Tarook, the Sea Gull, and though at first they were inclined to be angry at his sudden appearance, they soon saw that he had news to communicate, and so they crowded round him and begged him to speak. Tarook was a proud bird, and did not often leave his beloved sea; so they knew that something important must have brought him so far inshore.

He stood in their midst, dainty and handsome, with his snowy feathers and scarlet legs, and carefully brushed a fragment of grass from his wing before replying.

"Waga, the Fish-Hawk, came along this morning—in a shocking temper, too—and told me of your difficulties," he said. "Well, we of the sea know what has caused them!"

There was an instant hubbub. All the animals and birds cried out at once, saying, "What is it?" Tarook looked at them all calmly.

"If you make such a clatter, how can I tell you?" he asked crossly. "I have not much time either, because my mate and I have youngsters to look after, and it is nearly time I got back to find their dinner."

The animals became silent at once, and looked at him anxiously.

"Three nights ago," said Tarook, "Tat-e-lak, the big Frog, came out of the sea. Everyone knows he lives there, but none of us had ever seen him—and he is as large as many wurleys. All the sea was troubled at his coming, and big waves rolled in and beat upon the shore, so that we could scarcely see the rocks for spray. A hollow booming sound came from under the sea, and all our young ones were very much alarmed. Then a wave larger than all the rest put together crashed into the beach, and when it began to roll back we saw Tat-e-lak waddling up the shore. Most frogs hop, but he is so huge that he gets along in a kind of shuffle."

"But where did he go?" cried Kadin, the Inguana-lizard.

"He waddled away into the plains beyond, and when I flew in to look for him, for awhile I could not find him. Then I heard a strange noise of water sucking, and I flew to where it came from. There was a hollow in the creek bank, and Tat-e-lak was sitting there, with his head in the water, sucking it all up; and as he sucked, he swelled. It was not a nice sight, and soon I flew away."

"But where is he now? And what did he do?" asked the animals anxiously.

"I did not watch him anymore. But the West Wind knows all about him, and he told me when I was out fishing last night. It seems that Tat-e-lak lives under the sea, because of his former sins, and that is why he has grown so huge. But he always wants to come back to land, and sometimes he breaks away from his prison under the sea and gets up to the surface—and a great stir his coming makes: it's very annoying if you're fishing, for it scares all the fish away into the farthest corners of the rocks. But the salt water he has drunk for so long makes him terribly thirsty, and unless he can get fresh water to drink he has to go back to his sea-prison."

"Then that is why he has drunk all of ours!" cried the animals.

Tarook nodded very hard.

"Yes," he said. "It is very seldom that he gets a chance of coming up; and his last three landings have been made in the desert, where he has had no water at all, and has been forced to hurry back meekly to the sea. So he is now more thirsty than he ever was before. The West Wind says he did not stop drinking until this morning—and now there is no water anywhere, as you know."

"Then how shall we ever get anymore? Are we to die of thirst?"

"Well, that I do not know. I have told you all that I know," said Tarook. "Tat-e-lak is somewhere on shore, and so far as I can tell, all the water is inside him. But I do not know where he is, nor if you can do anything. Now I must go back to my young ones, for they will certainly be hungry, and my mate will be cross." He bowed to the Kangaroo, and flew up into the air. Then he went skimming over the forest to the sea.

When he had gone, the animals talked again, but there was great grief among them, and they did not know what to do. At last it was agreed that Malian, the Eaglehawk, should fly to the shore and find out anything he could about Tat-e-lak. So huge a Frog, they thought, could not hide himself from the eyes of an Eaglehawk, which can see even a little shrew-mouse in the grass as he flies. So Mirran, the Kangaroo, bade Malian be as quick as possible, and he flew off, while all the people awaited his return as patiently as they could. But they were too thirsty to be very patient.

It was evening when Malian returned. The day had seemed very long, and he was tired, for it is not easy to fly for a long while without water.

"Tat-e-lak is the most terrible Frog you could imagine," he said. "He is squatting on a rise not far from the sea, and he has drunk so much that he cannot move. His body is swelled up so that he is bigger than anything that ever existed: bigger than the little hill on which he sits. Nothing could possibly be so large as he is. He does not speak at all."

"But what is to be done?" cried the other animals.

"I asked everyone I met, but they could not tell me. So at last I found old Blook, the Bullfrog, for it struck me that he would know more of the ways of other Frogs than anyone else. I found him with great difficulty, and for a long time he was too angry to speak, for he has now no water to remain in, and none to drink. But he knows all about Tat-e-lak. He says that now he has inside him all the waters that should cover the waste places of the earth, but that we shall never have water unless he can be made to laugh!"

"To laugh!" cried the animals. "Who can make a Frog laugh?"

"Blook knows he cannot, so that is why he is angry," answered Malian. "But that is the only way. If Tat-e-lak laughs, all the water will run out of his mouth, and there will once more be plenty for everyone. But unless he laughs he will sit there for ever, unable to move; and soon we shall all die of thirst."

The animals talked over this bad news for a long time, and at last they agreed that everyone who could be at all funny must go and try to make Tat-e-lak laugh. A great many at once said that they could be funny; but when they were tried, their performances were so dull that most of those who looked on were quite annoyed, and refused to let them go near the Frog, for fear he should lose his temper instead of laughing. However, everyone was too thirsty to wait to try all those willing to undertake to make him merry: and they set off through the

Bush in a queer company, the animals running, hopping or walking, the snakes and reptiles crawling, and the birds flying overhead. "The water will run back to you before we do!" they cried to the wives and young ones they were leaving behind. But that was just a piece of brave talk, for in reality they did not feel at all sure about it. They hurried through the scrub, getting more and more scattered as they went along, for the swift ones would not wait for those who were slower. In the early morning the leaders came out of the trees, and found themselves on a swampy plain leading to the sea. All the water had dried up, and a creek that had its course through it was also dry. It was a very dreary-looking place.

Not far from the beach there was a little hill; and, sitting on it, they saw the monster Frog. He was a terrible creature in appearance, for he was so immense that the hill was lost under him, just like a hugely fat man sitting on a button mushroom. He was so swelled up that it seemed that if anything pricked him he would burst like a balloon; but when they came near him they saw how thick his skin was, and knew that no prick would go through it. His beady eyes were bulging out, and though they tried to attract his attention, he only gazed out to sea and took no notice of them at all.

"Well, he has certainly had a great drink, but he does not look as if he had enjoyed it," remarked Mirran, hopping round him.

"I should think he would find himself more comfortable under the sea than sitting on that poor little hill!" said Merkein, the Jackass.

"He will probably go back to the sea," the Native Companion answered. "Let us hope he will not take all the water with him."

"How uncomfortable he must be!—why, he is like a mountain!" hissed Mumung, the Black Snake. "May I not go and bite him?"

"Certainly not!" said Mirran hastily. "It might make him angry; or he might die, and we do not want the water poisoned. Unless you can make him laugh, you had better get into your hole!" So Mumung subsided, muttering angrily to himself.

Then the animals began to try to make the Frog laugh. It was the first circus that ever was in Australia. They danced and capered and pranced before him, and the birds sang him the most ridiculous songs they could think of, and the insects sat on his head and told him the funniest stories they had gathered in flying round the world: but he did not take the smallest notice of any of them. His bulging eyes saw them all, but not a word did he say.

It is very hard to be funny when nobody laughs, and the animals soon became rather disheartened. But Mirran would not let them stop. He himself did most wonderful jumps before the Frog, and once hopped right over the Emu, who looked so comical when she saw the great body sailing over her that all the animals burst out laughing; but the Frog merely looked as though he would like to go to sleep. Then Menak, the Bandicoot, brought his brothers, and performed all kinds of antics; and the 'Possums climbed up a little tree and hung from its boughs, and were very funny in their gymnastics; and the Dingo and his tribe held a coursing match round the hill on which the Frog sat, going so fast that no one could see where one yellow dog ended and the next began; but none of these things amused the Frog at all. He stared straight in front of him, and, if possible, he looked a little more bulgy. But that was all.

The animals held another council, and tried to think of other funny things. Mirran remembered how the Jackass had laughed when he had sat down on Kowern, the Porcupine, and though that had been a most unpleasant experience for him, he bravely offered to do it again. Kowern, however, did not like the idea, and scuttled away into a hole, and they had great difficulty in finding him—and when they did find him, it was quite another matter to make him come out. At last they induced him to appear, and to let Mirran sit on him. But it was not a successful experiment. Perhaps Mirran was nervous, for he knew how it felt to sit on Kowern's quills; and so he let himself down gently, and Kowern gave a heavy groan, but no one even smiled. As for the Frog, he was heard to snore. It was all rather hard on Mirran, for the experiment hurt him just as much as if it had been quite successful.

So the day went on, and when it was nearly evening, the animals could do no more: and still Tat-e-lak sat and stared stupidly before him, and looked more and more huge and bulgy in the gathering darkness; and Waat, the Red Wallaby, declared that the little hill he sat on was beginning to flatten under his weight. They were quite hopeless, at last. All were so tired and thirsty that they could not have attempted more antics, even had they known any, but, indeed, they had done everything they knew. They sat in a half-circle round the great Frog and looked at him sadly; and the Frog sat on his hill and did not look at anything at all.

Just about this time, Noy-Yang, the great Eel, woke up. He was lying in a deep crack in the muddy bed of the creek, and when the mud dried and hardened it pinched him, and he squirmed and woke. To his surprise, there was no water anywhere. Noy-Yang wriggled out of his crack, very astonished and indignant.

He found all the creek-bed dry, as you know; so he wriggled across it and up the bank, and came out on a little mud-flat by the sea. There he looked about him. On one side the sea rippled, but Noy-Yang knew that its water was no good for him. On the other was only dry land— the swampy ground he knew and loved, but now there was no water in it. It was very puzzling to a sleepy Eel.

He looked a little farther and saw the great Frog sitting on his hill. But he looked so huge that Noy-Yang thought the hill had simply grown bigger while he slept; and though that was surprising, it was not nearly so surprising as finding no water. Then he saw all the animals sitting about him, but he took no notice of them. All he cared for was to get away from this hot, dry mud, and find a cool creek running over its soft bed.

So he wriggled on, making very good time across the flat. Nobody saw him, for all the animals were looking miserably at the Frog.

Kowern, the Porcupine, had felt very sore and bruised after Mirran had sat on him for the second time. He was a sulky fellow, and he did not want to be sat on anymore, even if it were for the good of all the people. "Mirran will be making a habit of this soon," he said crossly; "I will get out of the way." So he hurried off, and got into the nearest hole, which happened to be near the edge of the mud-flat. There he went to sleep.

Noy-Yang came wriggling along, hating the hard ground, and only wanting to get to a decent creek. He was in such a hurry that he did not see Kowern, and he wiggled right across him—and it seemed to him that each of Kowern's spines found a different place in his soft body.

Noy-Yang cried out very loudly and threw himself backwards to get off those dreadful spikes. He was too sore to creep at all: the only part of him that was not hurt was the very point of his tail, and he stood up on that and danced about in his wrath and pain, with his body wriggling in the air, and his mouth wide open. And when the monster Frog caught sight of the Eel dancing on his tail on the mud-flat, he opened his mouth and let out such a great shout of laughter as had never been heard before in the world or will ever be heard again.

Then all the waters came rushing out of the Frog's mouth, and in a

MARY GRANT BRUCE

moment the dry swamp was filled with it, and a sheet of water rushed over the mud-flat where Noy-Yang was dancing, and carried him away—which was exactly what Noy-Yang liked, and made him forget all his sores. It was not so nice for Kowern, the Porcupine, for he was swept away, too, and as he could not swim, he was drowned. But he was so bad-tempered that nobody cared very much.

Tat-e-lak went on laughing, and the water kept pouring out of his open mouth; and as he laughed he shrank and shrank, and his skin became flabby and hung in folds about him. He shrank until he was only as large as a few ordinary frogs put together: and then he gave a loud croak, and dived off into the water. He swam away, and none of the animals ever saw him again.

At that moment the animals were much too busy with their own affairs to think much about Tat-e-lak. When the water first appeared they rushed at it eagerly, and each drank as much as he could. Then they felt better, and looked about them. Mirran, the Kangaroo, was the first to make a discovery.

"Ky! It will be a flood!" said he.

"A flood—nonsense!" said Warreen, the Wombat. "Why, ten minutes ago it was a drought!"

"Yes, and now it will be a flood," said Mirran, watching keenly. "Look!"

The water had run all over the plain, filling up the swamp, and already the creek showed like a line of silver where but a few moments ago there had been only dry mud. But it was plain that the water could not get away quickly enough. All the plain was like a sea, and there were big waves washing round the little hills.

"Save yourselves!" cried Mirran, to the people. "Soon there will be no dry land at all!"

He set off with great bounds, thinking of his mate and the little ones he had left in the forest. Behind him came all the people, running, jumping and crawling; and behind them came the water, in one great wave. Some reached the high ground of the forest first, and found safety, and others took refuge on hills, while those that could climb fled up trees. But many could not get away quickly, and the waters caught them, and they were drowned.

Next morning the animals who were saved gathered at the edge of the forest and looked over the flood. It stretched quite across the plain, and between it and the sea was only the yellow line of the sand-hummocks. Nearer to the forest were a few little hills, and on these could be seen forlorn figures, huddling together for warmth—for the air had become very cold.

"There are some of our people!" cried Mirran in a loud voice. "How are we to rescue them?"

No one could answer this question. None of the animals could swim, and if they had been able to do so, they had still no way of getting the castaways to dry land. They could only look at them and weep because they were so helpless.

After awhile, Booran, the Pelican, came flying up, in a state of great excitement.

"Have you seen them?" he cried. "Waat is there, and little Tonga, the 'Possum, and old Warreen, and a lot of others; and soon they will die of cold and hunger if they are not saved. So I must save them."

"You!" said all the animals.

"There's no need to say it in that tone!" said Booran angrily. "I can make a canoe and sail over quite easily. It will please me very much to save the poor things."

So Booran cut a big bark canoe, which he called Gre. He was very proud of it, and would not let anyone touch it or help him at all; and when it was finished he got in and paddled over to the little islands where the animals shivered and shook, with soaked fur and heavy hearts. They grew excited when they saw Booran coming, and when he arrived, with his canoe, they nearly tipped it over by all trying to get in at once. This was repeated at each island, and at last Booran lost his temper altogether and threatened to leave them all where they were. This dreadful idea made them very meek, and they were quite silent as Booran paddled them towards the shore.

Now, Booran had not a pleasant nature. It did not suit him to find people meek, for it at once made him conceited and inclined to be a bully. He felt very important, to be taking so many animals back in his boat; and so he began to say rude things to them, and in every way to be unpleasant. The animals bore this quietly for a time, for they were too cold to want to dispute with him, and besides, they were really very grateful for being saved. But after a while, he became so overbearing that Waat, the Red Wallaby, answered him back sharply, and others joined in. Before they got to shore, they were all quarrelling violently, and when they had only a few yards to go Booran suddenly stopped paddling, and jumped out so quickly that he upset the canoe, and threw

MARY GRANT BRUCE

all the animals into the water. He swam off, chuckling, and saying, "That will help to cool your bad tempers!"

The water was not deep, and the animals escaped with only a ducking. They struggled to the dry land, very wet and miserable.

"That was a mean trick to play on us," said little Tonga, his teeth chattering. "I would like to fight Booran, if only he would come ashore. But he will keep out of our way now."

"Ky! Look at him!" said Waat.

They looked, and they saw Booran coming in rapidly, as though he were floating on the water, and had no power to stop himself. His eyes were fixed and glassy, and his great beak wide open. A wave brought him right up on the shore, and blew over him in a cloud of spray. When the spray had gone, Booran had gone, too; and where he had lain on the bank was a big rock, shaped something like a pelican.

That was the story old Conara told me, as we fished for Murray cod together. He said that all his people knew the rock, and called it the Pelican Rock; and it stood on the plain long after Booran and his children's children's children were almost forgotten. Today the plain is dry, and no water ever lodges there; but when the blacks see the Pelican Rock they think of the time when it was all in flood, when Tat-e-lak, the great Frog, nearly caused all the animals to die of thirst, and when Noy-Yang, the Eel, saved them by dancing on his tail on a mud-flat by the sea.

VIII

The Maiden who found the Moon

Chapter I

Very long ago, before the white man came to conquer the land, a tribe of black people lived in a great forest. Beyond their country was a range of mountains which separated them from another tribe of fierce and warlike blacks, and on one side they were bounded by the sea. They were a prosperous tribe, for not only was there plenty of game in the forest, to give them food and rugs of skins for clothing, but the sea gave them fish: and fish were useful both to eat and for their bones. The blacks made many things out of fish-bones, and found them very useful for tipping spears and other weapons.

Being so powerful a tribe, they were not much molested by other blacks. The mountains to the north were their chief protection. No wandering parties of fighting men were likely to cross them and surprise the tribe, for they were steep and rugged and full of ravines and deep gullies that were difficult to cross, unless you knew the right tracks. The nearest tribe had come over more than once, and great battles had taken place; but the sea-tribe was always prepared, for the noise of their coming was too great to be hidden. There had been great fights, but the sea-tribe had always won. Now they were too strong to fear any attack. So strong were they, indeed, that they did not trouble about fighting, but only wished to be peaceful. Their life was a very simple and happy one, and they did not want anything better.

The tribe was called the Baringa tribe, and the name of its chief was Wadaro. He was a tall, silent man, very proud of his people and their country, and of his six big sons—all strong fighting-men, like himself—but most of all, he was proud of his daughter, Miraga.

Miraga was just of woman's age, and no girl in all the tribe was so beautiful. She was straight and supple as a young sapling, lissom as the tendrils of the clematis, and beautiful as the dawn striking on the face of the waters. Her deep eyes were full of light, and she was always merry. The little children loved her, and used to bring her blossoms of the red native fuchsia, to twine in her glossy black hair.

Most blacks, men and women, look on everything they meet with one thought. They ask, "Is it good to eat?" But Miraga was different. She had made friends with many of the little animals of the Bush, and they were her playmates: bandicoots, shrew-mice, pouch-mice, kangaroo-rats, and other tiny things. They were quite easy to tame, if anyone tried; even snappy little Yikaura, the native cat, with its spotted body and fierce sharp head, became quite gentle with Miraga, and did not try to touch her other pets. She begged the tribe not to eat the animals she loved, and they consented. Of course, in many tribes it would have been necessary to go on using them for food, and any woman who tried to save them would only have been laughed at. But the Baringa folk had so much food that they could easily afford to spare these little furry things. Besides, it was Miraga who asked, and was she not the chief's daughter?

However, it was not only because she was the chief's daughter that the people loved Miraga and did what she asked them. She was always kind and merry, and went about the camp singing happily, generally with a cluster of children running after her. If anyone were sick she was very good, bringing food and medicines. Being the daughter of Wadaro, the chief, she might have escaped all work; but instead, she did her share, and used to go out digging for yams and other roots with the other girls of the tribe, the happiest of them all.

The tribe beyond the northern hills was called the Burrin. They were very fierce and had many fighting-men; but their country was not so good as that of the Baringa, and they were very jealous of the happy sea-tribe. One time they came to the conclusion that it was long since they had had a fight—and that it would be a very good thing to try and win the Baringa country. They did not want to go over the mountains unprepared. So they sent a picked band of young men, telling them to cross into the land of the Baringas and find out if they were very strong, and if there were still much game in the forest. They were not to fight, but only to prowl in the forest and watch the sea-tribe stealthily. Then they were to return over the mountains with their report, so that the head-men of the Burrin could decide whether it were wise to send all their fighting-men over to try and conquer the Baringa.

The little band of Burrin men set off with great pride. Their leader was the chief's son, Yurong, who was stronger than any man of his tribe, and of a very fierce and cruel nature. He was not yet married, although that was only due to an accident. Once he had been about to take a wife, and had gone to her camp and hit her on the head with a waddy, which was one of the blacks' customs in some tribes, before carrying her to his own wurley. But he hit too hard, and the poor girl died—which caused Yurong a great deal of inconvenience, because her parents wanted to kill him too. It was only because he was the chief's son that he escaped with his life. Now he was still unmarried, because no girl would look at him. It made Yurong more bad-tempered than he was naturally, and that is saying a good deal. He had great hopes from the expedition into the Baringa country. If he came back successful, and won a name for himself as a fighter, he thought that all the maidens of his tribe would admire him, and forget that he had been so ready with his stick when he was betrothed first.

Yurong and his band left the plain where the Burrin tribe roamed, and journeyed over the mountains. They did not find any great difficulties, for they had been told where to find the best tracks, and they had scarcely any loads to hamper them. It was summer-time, and the lightest of rugs served them for covering at night, even in the keener air of the hills. There was no difficulty in finding food or water, and the stars were their guides.

When they came to the country of the Baringas they went very cautiously, for they did not wish to encounter any of Wadaro's men. In the daytime they hid themselves in gullies or in bends of the creek, only coming out when their scouts knew that no enemies were near; but at night they travelled fast, and before long they climbed up a great hill that lay across their path, and from its topmost peak they saw the gleaming line of the sea. Then, watching, they saw camp-fire smoke drifting over the trees; and they knew they had found Wadaro's camp.

They became more careful than ever, knowing that now was their greatest danger. Sometimes they hid in trees, or in caves in the rocks, all the time watching, and noting in their memories the number of the men they saw and the signs of abundance of game. There was no doubt that this was a far better country than their own, and they thirsted to possess it. At the same time they could see how strong the Baringas were. Even their womenfolk were tall and straight and strong, and would help to fight for their land and their freedom. The Burrin men used to see them when they went out to dig in the Bush, a merry, laughing band. Always with them was a beautiful girl with red flowers in her hair. Yurong would watch her closely from his hiding-place, and he made up his mind that when the fighting was over this girl should

MARY GRANT BRUCE

be the chief part of his share of the spoils. He was so conceited that he never dreamed that his tribe would not win.

But misfortune fell upon Yurong and his little band. They were prowling round the outskirts of Wadaro's camp one night when a woman, hushing her crying baby to sleep, caught a glimpse of the black forms flitting among the trees. She gave the alarm silently, and silently the fighting-men of the Baringas hurled themselves upon the intruders. There was no time to flee: the Burrin men fought fiercely, knowing that escape was hopeless. One by one, they were killed.

Yurong was the last left alive. He turned and ran, when the last of his comrades fell, a dozen Baringas at his heels. The first he slew, turning on him and striking him down; then he ran on wildly, hearing behind him the hard breathing of the pursuing warriors.

Suddenly the ground under his feet gave way. He fell, down, down, into blackness, shouting as he went; then he struck icy water with a great splash. When he came to the surface he could see the moonlight far above him, and hear the voices of the Baringa men, loud and excited. Then he went under once more.

On the river-bank, steep and lofty, the Baringas watched the black pool where Yurong had disappeared. There was no sign of life there. "He is gone," they said at last. "No man ever came alive out of that place. Well, it is a good thing." They watched awhile longer, and then turned back to the camp, where songs of victory were ringing out among the trees.

Chapter II

But Yurong did not die.

When he sank for the second time, he did it on purpose. The fall had not hurt him, and his mind worked quickly, for he knew that only cunning could save him. He swam under water for a few moments, letting himself go with the current. But presently a kind of eddy dragged him down, and he found himself against a wall of rock, which blocked the way, so that there seemed to be no escape. But even in his agony he remembered that so long as the current ran there must be some way out; and he dived deeply into the eddy. It took him through a hole in the rock, far under the water, scraping him cruelly against the edges; but still, he was through, and on the other side he rose, gasping. Here the river was wider and shallower, and not so swift. Yurong let it carry him for awhile; then he scrambled out on one side, and found a hiding-place under a great boulder. He rubbed himself down with rushes, shivering. Then, crouching in his hole, he slept.

When he awoke, he knew that now he should not lose a moment in getting back to his tribe. He had learned the fighting strength of the Baringas, with all else that he had come to find out; but, besides that, he had now the deaths of his comrades to avenge. And yet, three days later, Yurong was still in hiding near the enemy's camp. He had made up his wicked mind that when he went away he would take with him the beautiful girl he had so often seen in the forest with her companions.

Quite unconscious of her danger, Miraga went about her daily work. The sight of her, and the beauty of her, burned into Yurong's brain; often in the forest he dogged her footsteps, but the other girls were always near her, and he dared not try to carry her away. He knew now she was the chief's daughter, and he smiled to think that through her he could deal the cruellest blow to Wadaro, besides gaining for himself the loveliest wife in all the Bush.

But out in the scrub the girls clustered about Miraga, and in the camp the young men were never far from her. There was not one of them who would not have gladly taken her as his bride, but she told her father that she was too young to think of being married, and Wadaro was glad enough to keep her by his side. But Yurong, fiercely jealous, could see that there was one man on whom Miraga's eyes would often turn when he was not looking in her direction—a tall fellow named Konawarr—the Swan—who loved her so dearly that indeed he scarcely gave her a chance to look at him, since he so rarely took his gaze from her! He was the leader of the young fighting-men, and a great hunter; and Yurong thirsted to kill him, as the kangaroos thirst for the creeks in summer, when Drought has laid his withering hand upon the waters.

So five days went by. In the forest Yurong hid, living on very little food—for he dared not often go hunting—and always watching the camp; and Miraga, never dreaming of the danger near her, lived her simple, happy life. The children always thronged round her when she moved about the camp, and she would pause to fondle the little naked black babies that tumbled round the wurleys, tossing them in the air until they shouted with laughter. Yurong saw with amazement how the little animals came to her and played at her feet, and it impressed him greatly with a sense of the wealth of the Baringa tribe. "Ky!" he said to himself, "they are able to use food for playthings!" Never before had he dreamed of such a thing.

One evening the girls went out into the scrub, yam-digging, each carrying her yam-stick and dilly-bag—the netted bag into which the black women put everything, from food to nose-ornaments. Miraga's was woven of red and white rushes, with a quaint pattern on one side, and she was very proud of it, for it had been Konawarr's gift. She was thinking of his kind eyes as she walked through the trees, brushing aside tendrils of starry clematis and wild convolvulus, and finding a way through musk and hazel thickets. He had looked at her very gently when he gave her the bag, and she knew that she could trust him. She was very happy as she wandered on—so happy that she did not notice for a while that she had strayed some distance from the other girls, and that already the shadows were creeping about the forest to make the darkness.

"I am too far from camp," she said aloud. "I must hurry back, or my father will be angry."

She turned to retrace her steps, pausing a moment to make sure of her direction. Then, from the gloom of a tall clump of dogwood, something sprang upon her and seized her. She struggled, sending a stifled cry into the forest—but it died as a heavy blow from a waddy took away her senses. Yurong carried her swiftly away.

Day came, and found them still fleeing, Miraga a helpless burden in her captor's arms. Days and nights passed, and still they travelled northwards, across the rivers, the forest, and the mountains. They went slowly, for at length Yurong could carry the girl no farther, and at first she was too weak to walk much. Even when she grew stronger she still pretended to be weak, doing all in her power to delay their flight—always straining her ears in the wild hope that behind her she might hear the feet of the men coming to save her—led by Wadaro and by Konawarr. Somewhere, she knew, they were searching for her. But as the days went by, and no help came, her heart began to sink hopelessly.

Yurong was not unkind to her. He treated her gently enough, telling her she was to be his wife, but she hated him more and more deeply each hour. Thinking her very weak, he let her travel slowly, and helped her over the rough places, though she shrank from his touch. But he took no risks with her. He kept his weapons carefully out of her reach, and at night, when they slept, he bound her feet and hands with strips of kangaroo-hide, so that she might not try to escape.

Then they came to the topmost crest of the mountains, and below them Yurong could see the country of his people. At that, Miraga gave up all hope. They camped on the ridge that night; and for the first time she sobbed herself to sleep.

She woke up a while later, with a sound of little whispers in her ears. It was quite dark inside the wurley; but she heard a patter of tiny, scurrying feet, and a few faint squeaks. Miraga lay very still, trembling. Then a shrill little voice came, very close to her.

"Mistress—oh, mistress!"

"Who is it?" she whispered.

"We are your Little People," came the faint voice. "Lie very still, and we will set you free!"

On her hand, Miraga felt a patter of tiny feet, like snowflakes falling. They ran all over her body; she felt them down at her bare ankles, and near her face. She knew them now, though it was dark—little Padi-padi, the pouch-mouse, and Punta, the shrew-mouse, and Kanungo, the kangaroo-rat, with the bandicoot, Talka. They were all her friends—her Little People. Dozens of them seemed to be there in the dark, nibbling furiously at the strips of hide on her wrists and ankles.

How long the time seemed as she lay, trembling, in great fear lest Yurong should awaken! The very sound of her own breathing was loud in her ears, and the faint rustlings of the Little People seemed a noise that must surely wake the sleeping warrior. But Yurong was tired, and he slept soundly: and the Little People worked hard. At last the bonds fell apart and she was free.

Gliding like a snake, she crept out of the wurley, and ran swiftly into the forest that clothed the mountains. But scarcely had she gone when Yurong woke and found she was not there.

He sprang to his feet with a shout, grasping his weapons, and rushed outside. There was no sign of Miraga—but his quick ear caught the sound of a breaking twig in the forest, and he raced in pursuit. Again he heard it, this time so close that he knew she could not be more than a few yards away. Then he found himself suddenly on the edge of a great wall of rock, and there was no time to stop. He shouted again, in despair, as he fell—down, down. Then no more sounds came.

But just on the edge of the precipice three bandicoots came out of a heap of dry sticks, laughing.

"That was easily done," said one. "It was only necessary to jump up and down among the sticks and break a few, and the silly fellow made sure it was Miraga."

"Well, he will not make anymore foolish mistakes," said his brother. "But is it not surprising to find how simple these humans are!"

"All but our mistress," the first said. "Come—we must make haste to follow her, or else we shall have another long hunt. And nobody knows what mischief she may fall into, if we are not there to look after her!"

Chapter III

MIRAGA RAN SWIFTLY INTO THE heart of the forest, glancing back in terror, lest at any moment she should see Yurong. She heard him shout, and the crash of his feet in pursuit as he plunged out of the wurley; and for a moment she gave herself up for lost. He was so swift and so strong: she knew that she could never escape him, once he was on her track.

Another cry reached her presently, not so close. It gave her her first throb of hope that Yurong had taken the wrong turning among the trees. Still she was far too terrified to slacken speed. She fled on, not knowing where she was going.

A great mountain peak loomed before her, and she fled up it. It was hard climbing, but it seemed to her safer than the dark forest, where at any moment Yurong's black face might appear. Here, at least, she might be safe; at least, he would not think of looking for her in this wild and rugged place. Perhaps, if she hid on the mountain for a few days he would grow tired of looking for her, and go away, back to his own people; and then she could try to find her way home. At the very thought of home, poor Miraga sobbed as she ran: it seemed so long since the happy days in the camp by the sea.

The way was strange. She climbed up, among great boulders and jagged crags of rock. Above her the peaks seemed to pierce the sky. Deep ravines were here and there, and she started away from their edges: somewhere, water fell swiftly, racing down some narrow bed among the rocks. So she went on, and the moonlight grew stronger and stronger, until it flooded all the mountain. She fought her way, step by step, up the last great peak. And, suddenly, in the midnight, she came out upon a great and shining tableland: then she knew that in her journeyings she had found the Moon!

She wandered on, in doubt and fear—fear, not of this strange new land, but of the men she dreaded to find there. But for a long time she saw no people. Only in the dim hours, when the earth-world glowed like a star, but all the moon-country was dark, there came about her the Little People that she knew and loved—Padi-padi, and Punta, Talka and Kanungo. And because she was very lonely, and a lonely woman loves the touch of something small and soft, she took some of them up and carried them with her in her dilly-bag.

"How did you know I was lost?" she asked them.

"How did we know?" they said, laughing at her. "Why, all the forest sang of it! The magpie chattered it in the dewy mornings, and Moko-Moko, the Bell-Bird, told all about it to the creeks in the gullies. Moko-Moko would not leave his quiet places to tell the other animals, but he knew the creeks would carry the story. Soon there was no animal in all the Bush that did not know where you had gone. Only we could not tell your own stupid people, for they would not understand."

"And are they looking for me?" Miraga asked.

"They seek for you night and day. Your father has led a party of fighting-men to the east, and Konawarr has gone north with all his friends. They never rest—all the time they seek you. And the women are wailing in the camp, and the little children crying, because you are gone."

That made Miraga cry, too.

"Can you not take me back?" she begged. "I can go if you will show me the way."

But the Little People shook their heads.

"No, we cannot do that," they said. "We can help you, and we can talk to you, but we may not take you back. You must find the way yourself."

So Miraga wandered on through the Moon-Country. It was very desolate and bare, strewn with rocks and craggy boulders, and to walk long upon it was hard for naked feet. There were no rivers, and no creeks, but a range of mountains rose in one place, and were so grim and terrible that Miraga would not try to climb them. She found stunted trees, bearing berries, which she ate, for she was very hungry.

"Perhaps they are poisonous, and will kill me," she said. "I do not think that greatly matters, for I begin to feel that I shall never get home."

But the berries were not poisonous. Indeed, Miraga felt better when she had eaten them. Her strength came back to her, and her limbs grew less weary. She put some of the berries into her dilly-bag for the Little People. Then she set off on her wanderings again.

She did not know how long she had been in the Moon-Country, after a while. It seemed that she had never done anything but find her

MARY GRANT BRUCE

way across its rugged plains, seeking ever for the track back to the green Earth-World. So silent and strange was it that she began to think there was no living being upon it but herself and the Little People she carried with her.

One day, wandering along a rocky edge, she quite suddenly came upon the camp of the Man-Who-Dwells-In-The-Moon. She cried out in fear, and fled. But he was awake, and when he saw this beautiful girl, he rose and gave chase.

But Miraga was fleet of foot; and the Man-Who-Dwells-In-The-Moon was a fat man, and heavy: for, as the blacks know, he never goes hunting, as men do, but always sits down in the shadow of his mountains. Presently, he saw that the girl was escaping; she drew farther and farther ahead, running like a dingo, and already he was puffing and panting. So he stamped his foot and called to his dogs, and they came out of the holes of the hills—great savage brutes, lean and hungry-looking, of a dark colour. They came, running and growling, and sniffing angrily at the air. Their master waved his hand, and they uttered a long howl and followed swiftly after Miraga.

Now, indeed, she thought that her end had come. Mists swam before her eyes, and her feet stumbled: she, whose limbs were so lithe and strong, tottered like a weary old woman. Behind her, the long howls of the dogs woke terror in her heart. They drew nearer; almost she could feel their hot panting breath. But just as she was about to sink down, exhausted, the Little People in the dilly-bag chattered and called to her. "Mistress! Oh, Mistress!" they cried. "Let us out, that we may save you!"

She heard them, and fumbled with shaking fingers at the fastening of the bag. It slipped from her shoulders, and fell to the ground; and as it fell, the animals burst out and fled in many directions, some here and some there, squeaking and chattering. And when the fierce Dogs of the Moon saw them, they forgot to pursue Miraga, but turned and coursed swiftly after the animals.

Behind them the Man-Who-Dwells-In-The-Moon shouted vainly to them. There are no animals in the Moon-Country, and so the Dogs have no chance of hunting; but the sight of the scampering Little People woke their instincts, and they dashed after them wildly. They caught some, and swiftly slew them; others dodged, and leaped, and twisted, escaping into little rockholes, where the dogs could not follow them. The noise of the hunting and the deep baying of the Dogs echoed round the Moon and made thunder boom among the Stars.

But Miraga ran on, stumbling for weariness. She knew that the Dogs were no longer close upon her, but she dreaded to hear them again at any moment, for she did not see how such feeble Little People could keep them off for long. So she ran, and as she went, her tears fell for the little friends who had given their lives for her. At last, too tired to see where her stumbling feet had led her, she came to the brink of a great precipice, and fell down and down, until her senses left her.

But when she opened her eyes again, it was to meet those of Konawarr; and he was holding her in his arms and calling her name over and over, with his voice full of pity and love; and behind him were his friends—all the band who had been seeking her with him. They were all smiling to her, with welcome and joy on each friendly face. For in her fall she had come back to the dear Earth-World once more, and her sorrows were at an end.

So, when the tribes look up to the sky on moonlit nights and see the great shape that looms across the brightness, they say it is the mighty Man-Who-Dwells-In-The-Moon; who, like themselves, is black, but grown heavy and slothful with much idleness and sitting-down. The parents scare idle children with his name, saying that if they do not bestir themselves they, too, will become fat and useless like him. But Miraga used to tell her children another story, and when she told it her eyes would brim with tears. It was the story of the Little People she loved, who followed her to the Moon-Country, and there gave up their lives for her, saving her first from Yurong, and then from the teeth of the Dogs of the Moon. And the children would shiver a little, clustering more closely—all save little Konawarr, who would grasp his tiny boomerang and declare that he would kill anything that dared to hurt his mother.

The great dogs still crouch around the Man-Who-Dwells-In-The-Moon, waiting to do his bidding. You can see them, if you look closely—dark spots, near the huge figure in the midst of the brightness. They are the fierce Dogs that guard the lonely country in the sky: the Dogs that long ago hunted, howling, after Miraga the Beautiful, across the shining spaces of the Moon.

MARY GRANT BRUCE

IX

MIRRAN AND WARREEN

Mirran, the Kangaroo, and Warreen, the Wombat, were once men. They did not belong to any tribe, but they lived together, and were quite happy. Nobody wanted them, and they did not want anybody. So *that* was quite satisfactory.

Warreen was the first. All his tribe had been drowned in a flood, leaving him quite alone. So he found a good camping-place, where there were both shelter and water, and he made himself a camp of bark, which he called, in the language of his tribe, a willum. He was not in a hurry when he was making it, so he did it well, and no rain could possibly come through it. One side of it was a big rock, which made it very strong, so that no wind was likely to blow it away. Overhead a beautiful clump of yellow rock-lilies drooped gracefully. Not that Warreen cared for lilies; and this particular clump annoyed him, for the rock was too steep for him to climb up and eat the lily-roots.

He had been living there for some time, very lazy and contented, when one day Mirran appeared. At first Warreen thought he meant to fight, and that also annoyed him, because he hated fighting. But Mirran soon showed him that he only wanted to be friends; and then Warreen discovered that he was very glad to have some one with whom he could talk. So after the manner of men, they sat down and yarned all day.

Several times during the day Mirran said, "I must be going." But Warreen always answered, "Oh, don't go yet"; and they went on talking harder than ever. Night came, and Mirran said, "It is really time I made a move." Warreen said, "Why not stay the night? I can put you up." They talked it over for a while, and then it was quite too late for Mirran to go. So he stayed all night, and in the morning Warreen said, "Why not spare me a few days, now that you are here?" Mirran willingly agreed to this, for he had nothing to do, and he thought it very nice of Warreen to put the invitation that way.

They became great friends. Mirran was tall and thin and sinewy, while Warreen was very short and dumpy, and exceedingly fat. Also, he was lazy, and he liked having some one to help him get food, at which Mirran was very quick and clever.

Mirran also was the last of his tribe. The others had been killed by warlike blacks, and Mirran would have been killed also, but that he managed to swim across a river and get away into the scrub. He was very active and fleet of foot, and delighted in running, which was an exercise that bored Warreen very badly. Soon they made an arrangement by which Mirran did all the hunting, while Warreen dug for yams and other roots, and prepared the food, just as a woman does. It suited them both very well.

Mirran had one peculiarity that Warreen at first thought exceedingly foolish. He did not like to sleep indoors. It was summer time when he came, and he would not build himself a willum, but slept upon a soft bed of grass under the stars. If a cold night came, or even a rainy one, he rolled himself in his 'possum rug and slept just as happily. Warreen began by thinking he was mad. But as time went on he often slept outside with Mirran, himself, especially on those nights when they were talking very hard and did not want to leave off. Warreen used to grumble at the hardness of the ground, but he was really very much better for staying outside, in the fresh night-air. His little willum was a very stuffy place.

Sometimes he would think about the Winter, and say to Mirran:

"When are you going to build your willum?"

"Oh, there is plenty of time," Mirran would say.

"The cold weather will be here, and then what will you do?"

"Oh, I expect I shall have my camp ready in time. It will not take me long to build it, when the time comes."

"If you are not very careful, you will find yourself caught by the Winter, and you will not like that," said Warreen. But Mirran only laughed and talked about something else. He hated building, and was anxious to put it off as long as possible.

Warreen had a very suspicious mind, and it often made him believe very stupid things. He was the kind of man who was best living alone, because so often he got foolish ideas into his head about other people, and imagined he had cause for offence when there was really none at all. So he began to wonder why Mirran would not build a camp, and the thought came to him that perhaps he did not intend to build at all, but meant to take possession of his own willum. Of course, that was ridiculous, for Mirran was only lazy, and kept saying to himself, "Tomorrow I will build"; and when tomorrow came, he would say, "Oh, it is beautiful weather; I need not worry about building for a few days yet." So he went on putting it off, and Warreen went on being suspicious, until sometimes he felt sorry he had ever asked Mirran to live with him. But Mirran sang and joked, and hunted, and had no idea that Warreen was making himself uneasy by such stupid thoughts.

One night, clouds came drifting over the sky, after a hot day, and Warreen said, "I am not going to sleep outside tonight."

"I don't think it will rain," said Mirran. "It is much cooler out here."

"Yes, but one soon forgets that when one is asleep. I hate getting wet," said Warreen.

"Well, just as you like," Mirran answered. "For my part, I am too fond of the stars to leave them." So he spread his 'possum rug in a soft place, and lay down. In a few minutes he was fast asleep, and Warreen went off to bed feeling rather bad-tempered, though he could not have told why.

In the night, heavy rain came, and the air grew rapidly very cold. Mirran woke up, grumbled a little at the weather, rolled himself in his 'possum rug and crept into the most sheltered corner he could find by the rock, not liking to disturb Warreen by going into the willum. It was too cold to sleep, so he soon uncovered the ashes of their camp fire, and put sticks on it; and there he crouched, shivering, and wishing Warreen would wake up and invite him to sleep in the shelter.

But the rain came more and more heavily and a keen wind arose; and a sudden squall put out Mirran's fire. Soon, little channels of water were finding their way in every direction over the hard ground, so that Mirran became very wet and half-frozen. Then he noticed a red glow inside the willum.

"That is good," he said, joyfully, "Warreen is awake, and has made himself a fire. Now he will ask me to go and lie down in his hut."

He crouched close by the rock for a long time, thinking each moment that Warreen would ask him in. But no sound came, and after a while he came to the conclusion that Warreen could not know he was awake. So he got up and went over to the door of the willum and looked in. The little fire was burning redly, and all looked very cosy and inviting to poor, frozen Mirran. Warreen lay near the fire, and looked at him suspiciously.

"Ky! what a night!" said Mirran, his teeth chattering. "You were right about the weather, Warreen, and I was wrong. I have been very sorry for the last hour that my camp is not built. May I come in and sit in that corner?"

There was not much vacant space in Warreen's little willum, but it was quite big enough for two at a pinch. In the corner to which Mirran pointed there was nothing. But Warreen looked at him suspiciously, and grunted under his breath.

"I want that corner for my head," he said, at last. And he turned over and laid his head there.

Mirran looked rather surprised.

"Never mind; this place will do," he said, pointing to another corner.

"I want that place for my feet," Warreen said. And he moved over and laid his feet there.

Still Mirran could not understand that his friend meant to be so churlish.

"Well, this place will suit me famously," he said, pointing to where Warreen's feet had been.

But that did not please Warreen either.

"You can't have that place—I may want it later on," he said, with a snarl. And he turned and lay down between the fire and Mirran, and shut his eyes.

Then Mirran realized that Warreen did not mean him to have any warmth or shelter, and he lost his temper. He rushed outside into the wet darkness, and stumbled over a big stone. That was not a lucky stumble for Warreen, for all that Mirran wanted at the moment was a weapon.

He picked up the stone and ran back into the willum. Warreen lay by the fire and he flung the stone at him as hard as he could. It hit Warreen on the forehead, and immediately his forehead went quite flat.

"That's something for you to remember me by!" said Mirran angrily. "You can keep your dark little hole of a willum and live in it always, just as you can keep your flat forehead. I have done with you!"

He turned and ran out of the hut, for he was afraid that if he stayed he would kill Warreen. Behind him, Warreen staggered to his feet and caught hold of his spear, which leaned against the wall near the doorway. He did not make any reply, but he drove the spear into the darkness after Mirran, and it hit him in the back and hung there. Mirran fell down without a word. The light from the fire shone on him as he lay there in the rain, with the spear behind him.

Warreen laughed a little, holding by his door-post.

"I shall have a flat forehead, shall I?" he said. "Well, you will have more than that. Where that spear sticks, there shall it stick always, and it will be a tail for you. You will never run or jump without it again—and never shall you have a willum." Then he had no more strength left, so he crept back and lay beside his fire, while Mirran lay in the pouring rain.

No one saw Warreen and Mirran again as men. But from that time two new animals came into the Bush, and the Magpie and the Minah, those two inquisitive birds who know everything, soon found out their story and told it to all the black people. So everybody knows that Warreen, the Wombat, and Mirran, the Kangaroo, were once men and lived together. They do not live together now, nor do they like each other. The Wombat is fat and surly and lazy, and he lives in a dark, ill-smelling hole in the ground. His forehead is flat, and he does not go far from his hole; and he is no more fond of working for his living than he was when he lived in a willum as a man. The Kangaroo lives in the free open places, and races through the Bush as swiftly as Mirran used to race long ago. But always behind him he carries Moo-ee-boo, as the blacks call his tail, and it has grown so that he has to use it in running and jumping, and now he could not get on without it. He is just as quick and gentle as ever, but when he is angry he can fight with his forepaws, just as a man fights with his hands.

Other animals of the Bush have holes and hiding-places, but the Kangaroo has none. He does not look for shelter, but sleeps in the open air. It is difficult to see him, for when he is eating young leaves and grass his skin looks just the same colour as the trees, and you are sometimes quite close to him before his bright eyes are seen watching you eagerly. Then he turns and hops away, faster than a horse can gallop, in great bounds that carry him yards at every stride, with Moo-ee-boo, his long tail, thumping the ground behind him. He has learned to use it—to balance on it and make it help him in those immense leaps that no animal in the Bush can equal. So Warreen did not do him so bad a turn as he hoped when he threw his spear at him that rainy night long ago.

X

THE DAUGHTERS OF WONKAWALA

The Chief Wonkawala was a powerful man, who ruled over a big tribe. They were a fierce and warlike people, always ready to go out against other tribes; and by fighting they had gained a great quantity of property, and roamed unmolested through a wide tract of country— which meant that all the tribe was well-fed.

Wonkawala had not always been a chief. He had been an ordinary warrior, but he was fiercer and stronger than most men, and he had gradually worked his way up to power and leadership. There were many jealous of him, who would have been glad to see his downfall; but Wonkawala was wary, as well as brave, and once he had gained his position, he kept it, and made himself stronger and stronger. He had several wives, and in his wurleys were fine furs and splendid weapons and abundance of grass mats. Everyone feared him, and he had all that the heart of a black chief could desire, except for one thing. He had no son.

Five daughters had Wonkawala, tall and beautiful girls, skilled in all women's work, and full of high courage, as befits the daughters of a chief. Yillin was the eldest, and she was also the bravest and wisest, so that her sisters all looked up to her and obeyed her. Many young warriors had wished to marry her, but she had refused them all. "Time enough," she said to her father. "At present it is enough for me to be the daughter of Wonkawala."

Her father was rather inclined to agree with her. He knew that her position as the eldest daughter of the chief—without brothers—was a fine thing, and that once she married she would live in a wurley much like any other woman's and do much the same hard work, and have much the same hard time. The life of the black women was not a very pleasant one—it was no wonder that they so soon became withered and bent and hideous. Hard work, the care of many babies, little food, and many blows: these were the portion of most women, and might well be that even of the daughter of a chief, when once she left her father's wurley for that of a young warrior. So Wonkawala, who was unlike many blacks in being very fond of his daughters, did not urge that Yillin should get married, and the suitors had to go disconsolately away.

But there came a time when Wonkawala fell ill, and for many weeks he lay in his wurley, shivering under his fur rugs, and becoming weaker and weaker. The medicine-men tried all kinds of treatment for him, but nothing seemed to do him any good. They painted him in strange designs, and cut him with shell knives to make him bleed: and when he complained of pain in the back they turned him on his face and stood on his back. So Wonkawala complained no more; but the back was no better.

After the sorcerers had tried these and many other methods of healing, they declared that some one had bewitched Wonkawala. This was a favourite device of puzzled sorcerers. They had made the tribes believe that if a man's enemy got possession of anything that had belonged to him—even such things as the bones of an animal he had eaten, broken weapons, scraps of furs he had worn, or, in fact, anything he had touched—it could be employed as a charm against him, especially to produce illness. This made the blacks careful to burn up all rubbish before leaving a camping-place; and they were very keen in finding odd scraps of property that had belonged to an unfriendly tribe. Anything of this kind that they found was given to the chief, to be carefully kept as a means of injuring the enemy. A fragment of this description was called a wuulon, and was thought to have great power as a charm for evil. Should one of the tribe wish to be revenged upon an enemy, he borrowed his wuulon from the chief, rubbed it with a mixture of red clay and emu fat, and tied it to the end of a spear-thrower, which he stuck upright in the ground before the camp-fire. Then all the blacks sat round, watching it, but at some distance away, so that their shadows should not fall upon it, and solemnly chanted imprecations until the spear-thrower fell to the ground. They believed that it would fall in the direction of the enemy to whom the wuulon belonged, and immediately they all threw hot ashes in the same direction, with hissing and curses, and prayers that ill-fortune and disease might fall upon the owner.

The sorcerers tried this practice with every wuulon in Wonkawala's possession; but whatever effect might have been produced on the owners of the wuulons, Wonkawala himself was not helped at all. He grew weaker and weaker, and it became plain that he must die.

The knowledge that they were to lose their chief threw all the blacks into mourning and weeping, so that the noise of their cries was heard in the wurley where Wonkawala lay. But besides those who mourned, there were others who plotted, even though they seemed to be crying as loudly as the rest. For, since Wonkawala had no son, some other man must be chosen to succeed him as chief, and there were at least half a dozen who thought they had every right to the position. So they all gathered their followings together, collecting as many supporters as each could muster, and there seemed every chance of a very pretty fight as soon as Wonkawala should breathe his last.

The dying chief was well aware of what was going on. He knew that they must fight it out between themselves, and that the strongest would win; but what he was most concerned about was the safety of his daughters. Their fate would probably be anything but pleasant. Once left without him, they would be no longer the leading girls of the tribe, and much petty spite and jealousy would probably be visited upon them by the other women. Or they might be made tools in the fight for the succession to his position, and mixed up in the feuds and disputes which would ensue: indeed, it might easily happen that they would be killed before the fighting settled down. In any case it seemed to Wonkawala that hardship and danger were ahead of them.

He called them to him one evening, and made them kneel down, so close that they could hear him when he spoke in a whisper.

"Listen," he said. "I am dying. No, do not begin wailing now—there will be time enough for that afterwards. My day is done, and it has been a good day: I have been a strong man and my name will be remembered as a chief. What can a man want more? But you are women, and my heart is uneasy about you."

"Nothing will matter to us, if you die!" said Yillin.

"You may think so now," said the chief, looking at her with affection in his fierce eyes. "But my death may well be the least of the bad things that may happen to you. You will be as slaves where you have been as princesses. Even if I am in the sky with Pund-jel, Maker of Men, I shall be unhappy to see that. Therefore, it seems to me that you must leave the tribe."

"Leave the tribe!" breathed Yillin, who always spoke for her sisters. "But where should we go?"

"I have dreamed that you shall go to the east," said her father. "What is to happen to you I do not know, but you must go. You may fall into the power of another tribe, but I believe they would be kinder to you than your own would be, for there will be much fighting here after I have gone to Pund-jel. I think any other tribe would take you in with the honour that is due to a chief's daughters. In any case, it is better to be slaves among strangers than in the place where you have been rulers."

"I would rather die than be a slave here!" said Yillin proudly.

"Spoken like a son!" said the old chief, nodding approval. "Get weapons and food ready secretly, all that you can carry: and when the men are away burying me, make your escape. They will be so busy in quarrelling that they will not notice soon that you have gone; and then they will be afraid to go after you, lest any should get the upper hand during their absence. Go to the east, and Pund-jel will decide your fate. Now I am weary, and I wish to sleep."

So Yillin and her sisters obeyed, and during the next few days they hid weapons in a secret place outside the camp, and crammed their dilly-bags with food, fire-sticks, charms, and all the things they could carry. Already they could see that there was wisdom in their father's advice. There was much talk that ceased suddenly when they came near, and the women used to whisper together, looking at them, and bursting into rude laughter. Yillin and her sisters held their heads high, but there was fierce anger in their hearts, for but a week back no one would have dared to show them any disrespect.

At last, one evening, Wonkawala died, and the whole tribe mourned for him. For days there was weeping and wailing, and all the time the chief's daughters remained within their wurley, seeing no one but the women who brought them food. As the time went on, the manner of these women became more and more curt, and the food they brought less excellent, until, on the last day of mourning, Yillin and her sisters were given worse meals than they had ever eaten before.

"Our father spoke truth," said Yillin. "It is time we fled."

"Time, indeed," said Peeka, the youngest sister. "Did you see Tarnar's sneering face as she threw this evil food in to us?"

"I would that Wonkawala, our father, could have come to life again to see it," said Yillin with an angry sob. "He would have withered her with his fury. But our day, like his, is done—in our own tribe. Never mind—we shall find luck elsewhere."

After noon of that day the men of the tribe bore the body of Wonkawala away, to bury it with honour. The women stayed behind, wailing loudly as long as the men were in sight; but as soon as the trees hid them from view they ceased to cry out, and began to laugh and eat and enjoy themselves. They fell silent, presently, as the five daughters of Wonkawala came out of their wurley and walked slowly across the camp. They were muffled in their 'possum-rugs, scarcely showing their faces.

For a moment there was silence, and then one of the women said something to another at which both burst into a cackle of laughter. Then another called to the five sisters, in a familiar and insolent manner.

"Where do you go, girls?"

"We go to mourn for our father in a quiet place," answered Yillin haughtily.

"Oh—then the camp is not good enough for you to mourn in?" cried the woman with a sneer "But do not be away too long—there will be plenty of work to do, for you, now. Remember, you are no longer our mistresses."

"No—it is your turn to serve us, now," cried another. "Bring me back some yams when you come—then perhaps there will not be so many beatings for you!" There was a yell of laughter from all the women, amidst which Yillin and her sisters marched out of the camp, with disdainful glances.

When they drew near their hiding-place they kept careful watch, in case anyone had followed them. As a matter of fact, all the women were by that time busily engaged in ransacking their wurley, and dividing among them the possessions the sisters had not been able to carry away; so that they were quite safe. They collected their weapons and hurried off into the forest.

They had obeyed their father and gone east, and the burial-place was west of the camp, so they met nobody, and their flight was not discovered that night. The men came back to the camp in the evening, hungry and full of eagerness about the fight for the leadership of the tribe, and the women were kept busy in looking after them. The first fight took place that very evening, and though it was not a very big one, it left no time for anyone to wonder what had become of the five sisters. Not until next day did the tribe realize that they had run away; and then, as Wonkawala had foreseen, no one wanted to run after them. Certain young warriors who had thought of marrying them were annoyed, but they could only promise themselves to pursue and capture them when the tribe should again have settled down under new leadership.

The five sisters were very sad when they started on their journey, for the Bush is a wide and lonely place for women, and there seemed nothing ahead of them but difficulty and danger. They wept as they hurried through the forest, nor did they dare to sleep for a long time.

Only when they were so weary that they could scarcely drag themselves along, did they fling themselves down in a grassy hollow, where tall ferns made a screen from any prying eyes, and a stream of water gave them refreshment. They slept soundly, and dreamed gentle dreams; and when they awoke in the morning it seemed that a great weight had been lifted from their hearts.

"I feel so happy, sisters," said Yillin, sitting up and rubbing her eyes. "Our father came to me in my sleep, and told me to be of good courage and to smile instead of weeping."

"He came to me, also," said Peeka, "and told me there was good luck ahead."

"After all," said another of the girls, "what have we to fret about? It is a fine thing to go out and see the world. I am certain that we are going to enjoy ourselves."

"It will be interesting, at any rate," said Yillin. "But we must hurry onward, for we are not yet safe from pursuit—though I do not think it will come."

They made as much haste as possible for the next few days, until it seemed certain that no one was tracking them down; and with each dawn they felt happier and more free from care. They were lucky in finding game, so that they were well-fed; and on the fifth day they came upon trees loaded with mulga apples, which gave them a great feast. They roasted many of the apples and carried them with them in their food-bowls. Sometimes they came to little creeks, fringed with maidenhair fern, where they bathed; sometimes they passed over great, rolling plains, where they could see for miles, and where kangaroos were feeding in little mobs, dotted here and there on the kangaroo-grass they loved. Flocks of white cockatoos, sulphur-crested, flew screaming overhead, and sometimes they saw the beautiful pink and grey galahs, wheeling aloft, the sunlight gleaming on their grey backs and rose-pink crests. Then they went across a little range of thickly-wooded hills, where the trees were covered with flocks of many-coloured parrots, and the purple-crowned lorikeets flew, screeching—sometimes alighting, like a flock of great butterflies, on a gum-tree, to hang head downwards among the leaves, licking the sweet eucalyptus honey from the flowers with their brush-like tongues.

Sometimes, when they had lain very quietly through a hot noon-tide hour, they saw the lyre bird, the shyest bird of all the Bush, dancing on the great mound—twenty or thirty feet high—which it builds for its dome-shaped nest; mocking, as it danced, the cries of half the birds in the country, and waving its beautiful lyre-shaped tail. The magpie woke them in the dawn with its rich gurgling notes; the beautiful blue-wren hopped near them, proud of his exquisite plumage of black and bright blue, chirping his happy little song. They passed swamps, where cranes and herons fished, stalking in the shallows, or flew lazily away with dangling legs; and sometimes they heard the booming of the bittern, which made them very much afraid. At evening they would hear a harsh, clanging cry, and, looking up, they would see a long line of black swans, flying into the sunset. There were other birds too, more than any white boy or girl will ever know about: for these were the old days of Australia, long before the white men had come to settle the country and destroy the Bush with their axes. But there were no rabbits, and no thistles, for Australia was free from them until the white men came.

Gradually the daughters of Wonkawala lost all fear. They were perfectly happy, and the Bush no longer seemed lonely to them; they had enough to eat, they were warm at night, and so strong and active, and so skilled in the use of weapons, had their woodland life made them, that they did not seem to mind whether they met enemies or not. They often danced as they went on their way, and made all the echoes of the forest ring with their songs.

At last, one day, they found their way barred by a wide river which flowed from north to south. They could, of course, all swim; but it was not easy to see how to get their furs across. They were talking about it, wondering whether they could make a canoe or a raft, when they heard a friendly hail, and, looking across, they saw five girls standing on the opposite bank.

"Who are you?" shouted the strangers.

"We are the daughters of Wonkawala," they cried. "Who are you?"

"We are girls of the Wapiya tribe, out looking for adventures."

"Why, so are we, and we have found many." They shouted questions and answers backwards and forwards, until they began to feel acquainted. "What do you eat?" "What furs have you?" "What songs do you sing?" That led to singing, and they sang all their favourite songs to each other, beating two boomerangs together as an accompaniment. When they had finished they felt a great desire to travel together.

"It is really a great pity that the river flows between us," cried the daughters of Wonkawala. "How can we join you?"

The Wapiya girls laughed.

"That is quite easy," they answered. "This is a magic river, and when once your feet have touched it you will be Magic too. Dance straight across!"

"You are making fun of us," cried Yillin.

"No, indeed, we are not. We cannot cross to you, for on your side there is no Magic. But if you will trust us, and dance across, you will find that you will not sink."

This was hard to believe, and the sisters looked at each other doubtfully. Then Yillin took off her rug and handed it to Peeka.

"It will be easy enough to try, and at the worst I can only get a wetting," she said. "Follow me if I do not sink."

She went down to the water and danced out upon its surface. It did not yield beneath her; the surface seemed to swing and heave as though it were elastic, but it supported her and she danced across with long, sliding steps. Behind her came her sisters; and so delightful was it to dance on the swinging river-top that they burst into singing, and so came, with music and laughter, to the other side. The Wapiya girls met them with open arms.

"Ky! You are brave enough to join us!" they cried. "Now we can all go in quest of adventure together, and who knows what wonderful things may befall us!"

So they told each other all their histories, and they held a feast; and after they had all eaten, they danced off to the east together, for they were all so happy that their feet refused to walk sedately. Presently they came to an open space where were many tiny hillocks.

"This is Paridi-Kadi, the place of ants," said the Wapiya girls. "Here we have often come before, to gather ants' eggs."

"Dearly do we love ants' eggs," said little Peeka, licking her lips.

"And these are very good eggs," said the eldest of the Wapiya girls, whose name was Nullor. "But the ants defend them well, and those who take them must make up their minds to be bitten."

"Ants' eggs are worth a few bites."

"Certainly they are. Now let us see if you are really as brave as you say."

They attacked the hillocks with their digging-sticks, and unearthed great stores of plump eggs, which they eagerly gathered. But they also unearthed numbers of huge ants of a glossy dark green colour, and these defended their eggs bravely, springing at the girls and biting them whenever they could.

"Ky!" said Yillin, shaking one off her arm. "It is as well that these eggs are so very good, for the bites are certainly very bad. We have no ants like these in our country."

"Have you had enough?" asked Nullor, laughing.

"Enough bites, yes; but not enough eggs," said Yillin, laughing as well. "The eggs are worth the pain." She thrust her digging-stick into a hillock so energetically that she scattered earth and eggs and ants in all directions, and one ant landed on Nullor's nose and bit it severely—whereat Nullor uttered a startled yell of pain, and the daughters of Wonkawala laughed very much.

"Who is brave now?" cried little Peeka.

Nullor rubbed her nose with a lump of wet earth, which, as she was black, did not have such a curious effect as it would have had on you.

"I was taken by surprise," she said, somewhat shamefacedly. "And indeed, my nose is not used to such treatment, for I do not usually poke it into ants' nests!"

They ate all the eggs, and rubbed their bites with chewed leaves, which soon took away the stings; and then they danced away together. After a time, Yillin saw an eagle flying low, carrying something in its talons. She flung a boomerang at it, and so well did she aim that she broke its neck, and the great bird came fluttering down. It fell into a pool of water and Yillin jumped in to rescue its prey, for she could see that it was alive. It turned out to be a half-grown dingo, a fine young dog, which was too bewildered, between flying and drowning, to make any objection to being captured. Yillin secured it with a string which she plaited of her own hair and as much of Peeka's as Peeka was willing to part with, and fed it with bits of wallaby; and the dog soon became friendly and licked her hand.

"He is a lovely dog," she said, "and I will always keep him. I will call him Dulderana."

"I think he will be rather a nuisance," said Nullor. "Anyway, he will soon leave you and go back into the Bush."

"I do not think he will," Yillin said.

"Well, you cannot teach him to dance or sing," said Nullor, laughing, "so he will have to run behind us."

"Of course he will; and he will be very useful in hunting," said Yillin. "We should not have lost that 'possum yesterday if we had had a dog."

Dulderana very soon made himself at home, and became great friends with all the girls. It amused him very much when they danced, and though he could not dance himself, he used to caper wildly round them, uttering short, sharp barks of delight. But their singing he did not like at all, and when they began, he used to sit down with his nose pointing skywards, and howl most dismally, until the girls could not sing for laughing. Then they would pelt bits of stick at him until he was sorry. By degrees he learned to endure the singing in silence, but he never pretended to enjoy it.

One day, as they went along, they saw in the far distance a silvery gleam.

"What is that?" asked Yillin.

"It looks like the duntyi, or silver bush," said the Wapiya girls, doubtfully.

"That does not grow in our country," said Yillin. "Let us go and look at it."

But when they drew near, they saw that it was not a bush at all. Instead, it was a man, a very old man. He had no hair on his head, but his great silver beard hung straggling to his knees, and when the breeze blew it about it was so large that it was no wonder they had mistaken it for a bush. No word did he speak, but he sat and looked at them in silence, and when they greeted him respectfully he only nodded. Something about him made them feel afraid. They clustered together, looking at him. At last he spoke.

"I have come too soon," he said. "You are not ready for me yet. Go on."

At that Dulderana howled very dismally indeed, and rushed away with his tail between his legs. The girls quite understood how he felt, and they also ran away, never stopping until they were far from the strange old man.

"Now, who was that?" Yillin said.

Nullor looked uneasy.

"I do not know," she said. "This is a strange country, and there is much Magic in it. We will hurry on, or he may perhaps come after us."

So they hastened on into the forest, forgetting, for a while, to dance; but then their fear left them, and again their songs rang through the Bush. They passed a clump of black wattle, the trunks of which were covered with gum, in great shining masses, so that they had a splendid feast; for the gum was both food and drink, and what they could not eat they mixed with water and drank, enjoying its sweet flavour. With their bags filled with gum they went on, and one evening they camped among a grove of banksia trees, near a pool of quiet water. It was not very good water to drink, but the Wapiya girls showed the five sisters how to suck it up through banksia cones, which strained out any impurities and gave it a very pleasant taste. They were tired, and lay down early.

In the night a great wind sprang up, and with it came a curious booming noise. It woke the daughters of Wonkawala, and they sat up in alarm.

"Ky! that must be a huge bittern," said Peeka.

"It is not like a bittern," Yillin said. "I have never heard any sound like it. Perhaps it is the Bunyip, of whom our mother used to tell us when we were little—a terrible beast who lives in swamps, and whose voice fills everyone with terror."

The Wapiya girls woke up, and they also listened. Then they laughed among themselves, but they did not let the sisters see that they were laughing. They seemed to think little of the noise.

"It is only the wind howling," they said. "Lie down and sleep, you five inlanders!"

"What do you mean by that?" demanded Yillin. But the Wapiya girls only giggled again, and lay down, declaring that no Bunyip was going to spoil their sleep. And as they were so cheerful, the sisters came to the conclusion that they might as well do the same.

When they awoke it was day, and the booming was still going on, and the wind felt fresh and wet. The Wapiya girls were already up, and they greeted them with laughter.

"We have a surprise for you," said they. "Shut your eyes, and let us lead you."

The sisters did so, and felt themselves led forward. Presently the earth became soft and yielding under their feet, and they cried out in alarm, but the others laughed again, and said, "Never mind, you are quite safe."

In a moment more they said, "Now, open your eyes!" The sisters did so, and lo! they stood before a great sheet of water with high, tumbling waves. Blue and sparkling was the water, and the big waves came rolling in, gathering themselves up slowly with their tops a mass of foam, which slowly rose and curled over until it plunged down, crashing in a smother of breaking bubbles. The daughters of Wonkawala had never seen anything like it before, and they gasped in amazement.

"Ky! what a river!" they cried. "Where is the other side?"

The Wapiya girls shouted with laughter.

"The other side!" they gasped, when they could speak. "Why, there is no other side. This is the Sea, and it is the end of all things. Have you never heard of it?"

"Is *that* the Sea?" The five sisters stared. "We have heard stories of it from the old men and women, but we never imagined that it was like this. No one could imagine it without seeing it. Have you known it before?"

"Oh, yes. We have often camped here with our tribe. Come nearer."

They took the sisters down to the edge of the water, and presently a great wave rolled in, broke in a thunderous roar, and came dashing up the sand. The sisters stared at it in amazed admiration at first, and then, as it came nearer, Fear fell upon them, and they screamed and turned to fly. They ran as fast as they could in the yielding sand, but the wave came faster and the water caught them, at first round their ankles and then swiftly mounting to their knees. Then it went back, and the sisters thought that they were slipping back with it, and screamed louder than ever. The Wapiya girls, themselves weak with laughter, caught hold of them.

"The Sea!" screamed the sisters. "The Sea is carrying us away!"

The others led them up on higher sand and laughed at them until they began to laugh at themselves.

"Never before have I seen water that runs backwards and forwards, as though a great giant were shaking it in a bowl," said Yillin. "We are sorry to have been afraid, but it is all very peculiar and unexpected. Are you sure it is not Magic?"

"I do not think anyone can be sure of that about the Sea," said Nullor. "It is strange water, and indeed I often think that it is very great Magic indeed. But if it is, it is a good Magic, and we are not afraid of it."

"And this queer yellow earth, that slips away under the feet—is that Magic too?"

"Oh—the sand. Perhaps it is—who knows. But it will not hurt you. Come on, let us bathe in the Sea, for that is one of the most beautiful things in the world."

The daughters of Wonkawala hung back at first, for they were very doubtful of trusting themselves to the magic water. But the others laughed and persuaded them, and they ventured in, paddling at first, until they became used to the rushing breakers. But soon they gained confidence, and before long not even the Wapiya were bolder than they, and they would dive into a breaker and be carried in on its curling top, laughing and playing like so many mermaids: so that the Wapiya girls soon lost any feeling of superiority, and only regained it once, when Peeka, feeling thirsty, scooped up some of a passing wave in her cupped hands and took a deep draught. For the next two minutes Peeka was coughing and spluttering and spitting, while the other girls yelled with laughter.

"That is certainly very bad Magic," said Peeka angrily, when she could speak. "What has made the water turn bad?"

That set the Wapiya girls off into fresh peals of mirth, and it was some time before they could explain that the water was always salt. Peeka was annoyed, but presently she laughed too.

"Oh, well, if that is the worst of its Magic, there is not much to grumble at," she said. "Come on, girls, let us dive into this next one!" And the next moment Peeka's merry black face was half hidden in the flying spray as the breaker bore her ashore.

They stayed by the Sea for some days, for the inland girls were too fascinated to leave it, and when they were not bathing in it, they were wandering along the shore, wildly excited over finding shells and seaweed and all the other treasures of the sands. Then one day a great black cloud came up, obscuring all the sky, and instead of being sparkling blue and silver, the water turned to a dull grey and looked dead and oily. The other girls were afraid of it, and would not go into the cold, dark breakers: but Yillin, who loved bathing more than any of them, would not be persuaded, and plunged in for a swim. She did not stay long, for the water felt more and more uncomfortable each moment; so she let a big, sullen breaker carry her in, and, wading out, ran up the beach to the other girls.

They started back when they saw her, looking at her with amazement and fear.

"What have you done to yourself?" cried Nullor.

"I? Nothing. What are you looking at?"

Nullor pointed a shaking forefinger at her body, and looking down, Yillin uttered a bewildered cry. No longer was she smooth-skinned and black. Her body and legs were thickly covered with shining scales, so that she gleamed like silver.

"It is the water!" she stammered. "It must be!"

"Does it feel pleasant?" inquired Nullor. "It looks quite beautiful."

"I do not feel anything at all," Yillin answered. "But it certainly does look well." She gazed at her shining self with interest, and turned round

MARY GRANT BRUCE

so that the others might see if her back were similarly ornamented. It was, and the other girls grew a little jealous.

"Jump in, and see if the Magic will come upon you, too," cried Yillin.

They did not lose a moment. Flinging their fur aprons from them, they rushed down the beach and plunged into the dark waves. And lo! when they emerged, they too were covered with silver scales. They stood together on the sand, a shining company.

"Let us walk along the shore, and see what else will befall us," said Yillin.

They gathered up their property and set off eastwards again. The shore curved out after a time, forming a rocky cape. They rounded this, and found themselves on the coast of a little bay, round which they hurried, anxious to explore some great rocks at the farther point. But when they reached them, they found their way barred. The rocks were a solid wall: a great black cliff that rose sheer from the water, running far out beyond even the farthest line of the breakers. Nowhere was there any way of advancing: the bay was ringed with the dark, smooth cliffs. The little dog Dulderana whimpered as if in fear.

"Let us go back!" said the Wapiya girls. "This is not a good place."

For a moment the daughters of Wonkawala were inclined to agree. Then there came to them suddenly the vision of their father, who had said, "Go to the east," and they knew they must obey.

"We are not afraid," they said. "Go you back, if you wish."

"We do not wish to leave you," the Wapiya said sadly.

"Nor do we wish to lose you, for we have loved you very much," said the sisters. "But we must go forward. Will you not come?"

The Wapiya girls shook their heads.

"No," they said. "Something tells us that we must return, and never see you more. But we will always watch for you, and perhaps some day we may hear you coming, singing our old songs, and we will run to meet you."

They embraced each other, weeping, and slowly the Wapiya girls went back until the rocky promontory hid them from sight. Then Yillin dashed her tears away.

"Come, my sisters!" she cried.

They took hands and danced together towards the wall of rock that loomed before them, black, unbroken, forbidding. Yillin was at the end, and as she reached the rock she raised her Wona, or digging-stick, and struck the rock. It split open, and they danced through the cleft. Before them was no more the Sea, but a green country dotted with trees, and covered with thick grass. A little way from them was a low mound, towards which they danced. As they drew near, they saw that some one was sitting on it—a very old man, whose silver beard swept below his feet. He sat motionless, save that his hands were always busy, pulling the long silver hairs from his beard and twisting them into a cord.

"It is the old man we met long ago!" whispered the sisters.

Somehow, the fear that they had felt when they met him with the Wapiya girls was upon them no longer: and the little dog Dulderana, who had fled from him howling, now ran up to him gaily, frisking round him. The old man put out his hand and fondled him, and Dulderana snuggled against him; then, nestling down with his head on his fore-paws, he looked at Yillin as if to say, "This is my master."

Yillin understood the look in his eyes.

"Do you like him, Master?" she asked. "We bring him to you as a gift."

"That is a good gift," said the old man, looking much pleased. "And you are welcome, my children. I think that this time I have not met you too soon. Are you weary with all your wanderings?"

"No, we are never weary," said Yillin. "We have danced, and hunted, and bathed, and sung; and we have forgotten all our sorrows. Our father, Wonkawala, bade us come east, and we obeyed him."

"And so you found friends and happiness," said the old man. "Sit down, and tell me of all that you have seen."

They sat down in a semi-circle before him, and, speaking one after another, they told him the story of their long journey. He heard them in silence, nodding now and then: and all the time his fingers moved ceaselessly, plaiting the silver hairs into a long cord. It lay in great shining coils at his feet. The little dog nestled beside him, and sometimes, when he paused to adjust a fresh coil, his fingers rested for a moment on its head.

He smiled at the sisters when they had finished their story.

"It was indeed a great journey; and the Sea has clothed you in silver, so that you are more glorious than any chief's daughters have ever been before," he said. "And now comes the greatest adventure of all."

He rose, as he spoke, pointing to the sky. The sisters looked up, and cried out in awe. For as they looked, the clouds parted, and they saw behind them Arawotya, who lives in the sky: a great and gentle Being whose face seemed to have light behind it. He looked down at them kindly, and beckoned. Then he began to lower a long cord, made, like that of the old man, of plaited hair. It reached almost to the top of the mound where they stood.

"You are to go up," said the old man. "You first, I last of all. But first we will send up the little dog, that you may see how safe it is."

He took his silver cord and tied it round the body of Dulderana, then joining it to the magic cord from the sky. Then Arawotya pulled it up, so gently that the little dog never seemed frightened, and he disappeared behind a cloud. Presently the cord came back again, and one after another the old man tied the girls with it, and Arawotya drew them up to himself. Yillin was the last of the sisters to go, but as she was being pulled up she cut her hand with her digging-stick, and her Pirha, or food-bowl, fell. It was a very beautiful carved Pirha, and, because it had been her father's, Yillin felt very sad. Even when Arawotya had gently received her, and, untying the cord, placed her by her sisters, she peered over the edge of the cloud, trying to see where it had fallen.

The old man was being drawn up, and just as he reached the clouds Yillin caught sight of her Pirha, lying on the mound.

"See!" she whispered to Peeka. "My Pirha—it lies below. I will just slide down the cord and get it, for it belonged to our father, Wonkawala. Arawotya will forgive me and pull me up again."

She slid hurriedly down the cord and joyfully seized the bowl. But when she turned to climb up again she uttered a cry of despair, for the cord was out of her reach. Arawotya had drawn it up. As she looked, it disappeared, and then the cloud-masses swept together, blotting out everything above. She was alone.

All that day and night Yillin lay on the mound, weeping, and begging Arawotya to forgive her and take her up to her sisters. But all the clouds had gone, and there was only a clear blue sky, bright with moonlight and dotted with a million stars: and there was no sign of those whom she had lost. She gave herself up to despair.

"Yakai!" she moaned. "Better that I had remained a slave in the camp of Wonkawala than have come to this lonely land to die!"

Towards morning, exhausted, she fell into a troubled sleep. And in her sleep her father came to her, and his face was grave and kind.

"Alas, my daughter!" he said. "You have lost your chance of happiness for the sake of a worthless Pirha. What! did you imagine that you would need a Pirha in the sky?"

"No—but because it was yours, my father," she sobbed in her sleep.

Wonkawala's face shone with a great light.

"Always you were my dear and faithful daughter," he said. "Because of that, there is yet happiness for you. Go forward, and no matter what shall befall you, be of good courage."

Then the vision faded, and after that Yillin's sleep was no longer troubled. She woke refreshed in the morning, and although she was lonely for her sisters, there was hope in her heart. She took her weapons and went forward.

It was a quiet country. There seemed no men and women in it, nor even any animals; and even the birds were strange to her. She passed over a great rocky plain, making for a green line of trees that seemed to mark the windings of a creek, for she was very thirsty. She found it, a clear wide stream, and drank deeply: then she wandered along its banks. And here at length there was a touch of home, for there were many crimson parrots in the trees, and the noise of their harsh crying to each other was as music in her ears. They had their mates, and to see them made her feel less lonely.

She found some roots and berries, which she ate, hoping they were good for food: and when night came, she curled into a hollow under a rock and slept deeply, waking refreshed, eager to go on her way. Then for many days she wandered, following the course of the creek, for she was afraid to go far from water. She was a strange figure in her silvery scales. Whenever she caught sight of herself, mirrored in the water as she bent to drink, it gave her a new throb of amazement.

She was wandering along one day when a rustling in the bushes made her glance aside. To her surprise, a dog was looking at her, and she could see that it was a tame one. Yillin had always loved dogs, and she whistled to this one, trying to coax it to play with her. But the dog was suspicious, and backed away from her, growling: then it uttered a few short barks and raced off into the scrub.

Two black hunters, who were ranging through the Bush a little way off, stopped, hearing the barking.

"My dog has started game of some kind," said one. "He does not bark for nothing."

"Let us go and look," said the other. They turned aside in the direction of the sound, and presently came upon the dog, who bounded to his master and licked his hand.

"What have you been barking for?" demanded his master, patting him. The dog wagged his tail vigorously and ran a few paces into the bushes.

"I believe there is something in that direction," the hunter said. "We might as well go and see, Chukeroo."

They moved noiselessly through the scrub, and presently Chukeroo caught his friend's arm.

"See, Wonga," he whispered. "There is a demon! Let us fly!"

Wonga looked, and saw a strange, glittering figure standing by a tree. He was just as afraid as his friend, but he was also full of curiosity.

"It seems to be a woman-demon," he whispered back. "See! it has long hair, and the face is the face of a woman." He pondered, watching the strange apparition. "And it carries weapons—strange, that a demon should go armed, Chukeroo. I should like to get hold of those weapons. They would be worth having in a fight."

"You may try, if you like, but I have no fancy for fighting demons," said Chukeroo.

"I do not know that I have, either," said Wonga. "Perhaps, though, a woman-demon would not be so terrible to fight. Look how she glitters when she moves! She would be a startling wife for a man to take home to his wurley, Chukeroo."

"Everyone to his fancy," returned his friend. "Personally I prefer mine black."

"You are used to yours, but I have none yet," said Wonga, laughing, for he was a cheerful youth. "Come, I am going to get a nearer look at the demon. Are you afraid?"

"Very much, but I suppose I had better come," said Chukeroo grumblingly. "You are a mad-headed fellow, Wonga, and you will get into trouble if you do not take care. I only hope that this is not the sort of demon that the sorcerers tell us about, who can blast men to cinders with a wave of the hand."

He followed his friend, and they crept through the bushes until they found a place where they could see the strange being more closely. In their excitement they had forgotten the dog, and suddenly it gave a loud bark. The shining figure turned sharply and ran towards them.

"Save yourself!" uttered Chukeroo. "It has seen us!"

They turned to run, but in crossing a clear space Chukeroo caught his foot in a trail of clematis and fell headlong, scattering his weapons. Wonga pulled himself up, and raced back to help his friend. Before they could gather all the fallen spears the strange being was upon them.

Yillin was as astonished as the black hunters—and as afraid. But she had learned to defend herself, and so she flung her digging-stick at Wonga. It grazed his leg, and made him so angry that he forgot all about being afraid of this demon, and hurled his spears at her. But his fear returned when he saw them glance off her shining scales as though she were covered with glass, and then fall harmlessly to the ground. Chukeroo joined in the fight: but though the aim of both hunters was true, nothing seemed to pierce those magic scales. Moreover, the strange being, having lost her digging-stick, picked up the fallen spears and flung them at their owners so rapidly that they thought themselves lucky in being able to dodge behind trees with whole skins.

"She is indeed a demon!" gasped Chukeroo.

"She may be, but she is very like a woman," said Wonga. "And I am not going home to tell the other warriors that a woman has stolen my spears, even if she does happen to be a demon. Besides, you know as well as I do that they will not believe us. Even your own wife will laugh at you, and she will not believe."

"That is true enough," said Chukeroo gloomily. "What are we to do?"

"I will make you armour," said Wonga. "Then we will go back, and when the demon throws the spears at you they will stick in the armour, and I will rush in and secure them."

"I do not know that it is much of a plan, but at least I have no better," said Chukeroo. "Be quick, or the demon may come and find us unarmed."

So Wonga broke off young saplings, and lashed them round his friend with strips of twisted stringy bark fibre, until nothing of him could be seen, and he had great difficulty in moving. Then, slowly and cautiously, they made their way back to the open space where they had fought.

Yillin was standing wearily by a tree with the spears in her hand. She jumped round as they came, and while she flung spear after spear at Chukeroo, Wonga ran through the trees and came behind her. His foot struck against her own digging-stick, and he picked it up and rushed at her. The point caught in her shining scales, and ripped them up as though they were paper. They fell in tatters about her.

"Do not kill me!" she cried. "I am a chief's daughter!"

"A chief's daughter, are you?" said Wonga. Suddenly his angry face grew soft with pity. "Why, I thought you a demon," he said—"and lo! you are only a poor, frightened little girl!"

MARY GRANT BRUCE

So the wanderings of Yillin came to an end, and though she missed happiness with Arawotya in the sky, yet, as Wonkawala had said in her vision, she found it elsewhere. For Wonga took her home and married her, and his tribe treated her with honour because she was the daughter of a mighty chief; and later on, Wonga became the chief of his own tribe, and she helped him to rule it in wisdom. Very often she was lonely for her four sisters, especially for little Peeka, whom she had loved best of all: but she comforted herself by thinking that they were happy with Arawotya in the sky, and that some day she would find them again. Then, together, they would go at the last to Pund-jel, Maker of Men, and join their father Wonkawala. There were five stars in the southern sky that she liked to watch, for she grew to believe that they were her sisters, and that the tiniest of the five was her little dog Dulderana. They are the stars of the Southern Cross. And it seemed to Yillin that they looked down at her and smiled.

Otherwise, Yillin was never lonely, for many children came to her and Wonga, and her wurley always seemed full of jolly black babies and wee lasses and lads. Yillin did not mind however many there were, especially as she did not have to worry about clothes for them. They grew into strong, merry boys and girls, who loved dancing and songs and laughter just as she had always loved them. She used to tell them the story of her wanderings, and when she came to the part about the silver scales that had once covered her, they would pretend to hunt for them on her black skin, and would laugh very much because they could never find any. And Wonga would laugh too, and say, "Ah, well, many men find their wives demons after they have married them, so I was lucky in only thinking that of mine beforehand—and then finding I had made a mistake!"

XI

The Burning of the Crows

No one in the Bush ever had a good word to say for the Crows. From the very earliest times they were a noisy, mischievous race, always poking their strong beaks into what did not concern them, and never so happy as when they were annoying other people. Whatever a mother Crow taught her chickens, civility and good manners were not included in the lessons; they were accomplishments for which none of the family had the slightest use.

It did not at all trouble the Wokala, as the Crows were called, that they were unpopular. Indeed, they rather gloried in the amount of ill-feeling they were able to excite among the Bush folk. They were powerful birds, well able to hold their own in any quarrel with birds of their own size, and so quick and daring that they would even steal from animals, or attack weak ones, secure in the advantage given them by their strong wings. They made so many enemies, however, that they took to going about in flocks, so that no one dared molest them—not even Wildoo, the Eagle, or Kellelek, the Cockatoo.

Especially did Wildoo hate the Wokala. He was always proud, as the King of the Birds has every right to be, and among all birds that fly his word was law. He liked to keep good order, and if any bird displeased him, a few quiet words, possibly accompanied by a discreet peck, or a blow from one of his great wings, was more than enough to bring the offender to his senses. One day he had occasion to punish one of the Wokala, who had stolen the meal laboriously provided by the wife of Wook-ook, the Mopoke, for her husband, who was ill. The Wokala, battered and furious, flew away and told his story to the other Crows; who, equally furious, flew in a mob to the high crag where Wildoo had his nest. There was no one there, for it was too late in the season to find chickens: so the Wokala amused themselves by scattering the nest to pieces, and when Wildoo and his wife came home from hunting they hid among the bushes and screamed all sorts of insulting things at them. Wildoo took no notice, openly. It would have been beneath his dignity to go hunting smaller birds in thick bushes—which the Wokala very well knew. He merely folded his wings and, with his wife, perched on the edge of the rocky shelf where his nest had been, and stared out across the tossing green sea of gum-trees that clothed the rolling hills below, his yellow eyes full of silent anger. Gradually the Wokala grew tired of screaming, and, becoming hungry, flew away.

After that the Wokala became more insolent than ever. Even Wildoo was afraid of them, they said; and they kept together in a mob, and lost no chance of being rude to him. More and more they attacked and insulted the other birds, until no one felt safe if there were any chance of the evil Wokala coming near. Again and again complaints came to Wildoo of their wicked doings, and Wildoo heard them in silence, nodding his head, with his brain busy behind his yellow eyes. But he said nothing: until at length the other birds began to ask themselves was it really true that Wildoo was afraid? Wildoo was not at all afraid of a flock of squawking Wokala. But he was very much afraid of being made to look ridiculous. He had no intention of making a false step, and he did not quite know what to do. There was no one for him to talk to, for the Eagle is a lonely bird—not like Chirnip, the Magpie-Lark, or Tautani, the Cormorant, with dozens and dozens of friends. He is a king, and therefore he is lonely: and, being naturally silent, he does not talk much, even to his wife. All by himself he had to think out the problem of what to do about the Wokala; and, meanwhile, the Wokala perched above his nest and insulted him, and dropped bits of stick down upon his rocky shelf, and screamed rude things at his wife, until she said crossly to Wildoo, "I cannot think why you do not make an end of those abominable little white birds. They are a disgrace to any decent Kingdom, and you have not the spirit of a Bandicoot!" This annoyed and hurt Wildoo, but he said nothing—only looked at her until she caught a gleam of fire in the depths of his yellow eyes.

Perhaps you did not know that in the very early times all the Wokala were white? They were the whitest of all the birds of the Bush, without a single grey or coloured feather in all their bodies: so that there was a saying in the Bush, "As white as a Wokala." They were very proud of it, too, and thought it quite a disgrace if one of their chickens showed a sign of being even creamy in colour, once he was nearly fledged. They kept themselves very clean, going often to bathe; and when they flew about in a flock their dazzling whiteness almost hurt the eye, while, if they perched in a dead gum-tree, they looked like big snowflakes against the grey branches. Even Kellelek, the Cockatoo, was dingy compared to the gleaming whiteness of the Wokala. Somehow, it seemed to make their bad behaviour worse, since no one would expect a beautiful bird like polished marble to have the manners of a jungle pig.

Summer ended early that year, with a great thunder-storm, followed by a month of wild wind and driving rain: and all the birds were rather uncomfortable because the moulting season was scarcely over. Most of all, the Wokala were annoyed. They liked their white feathers so much, and were so proud of their smart appearance, that they always delayed moulting as long as ever they could; and now the bad weather caught them in a worse state than the other birds. When the rains ended, early frosts came, and found the Wokala without any of their new feather cloaks ready. They used to huddle together among the thickest trees, shivering and untidy.

In that part of the country there is a great black ironstone hill, treeless and forbidding. Few birds go there, for there is nowhere to perch, and but little food except the tiny rock-lizards that sun themselves in the hot mornings. Wildoo knew it well, for he often flew over it, and occasionally he was accustomed to stand on a shelf at the mouth of a cave near the top—a black hole in the hillside where no one but an Eagle would willingly perch alone. He took refuge in the cave one morning, during a fierce hail-storm; and it was there that an idea came to him.

That night as he came flying homewards, he brought in his great talons a bundle of dry sticks, and as he flapped his way over the black ironstone hill, he dropped down on the ledge and made a heap of his sticks on the floor of the cave. The next morning he did the same: and so it went on for many days, until he had a big pile of smooth sticks, something like a great nest. His wife came with him one evening, and was very much amused.

"Why have you taken to playing with sticks?" she asked, laughing. "I never saw such a funny heap. Is it a game?" But Wildoo only looked at her sourly, and said, "Be quiet, woman!" after the manner of husbands: and since she was more sensible than most wives, she was quiet.

It was after his heap of sticks was ready that Wildoo went to look for the Wokala. They had been far too uncomfortable lately to continue to be rude to him, and, in fact, were keeping out of the way of everyone; so that he had some difficulty in finding them, and might have given it up but for Corridella, the Eagle-hawk, who remembered having seen them near a sheltered gully between two hills.

"They are cold," said Corridella, laughing, "oh, so cold, and so sorry for themselves. There is no impudence left in them."

"Cold indeed must be the night that chills the impudence of the Wokala," said Wildoo.

"It is going to be a very cold night," said Corridella. "Already there is a sharp nip of frost in the air. I think that some of the Wokala will be dead before morning, for none of them have their new feather cloaks nearly ready." He chuckled. "Well, no one in the Bush will mourn for them. Perhaps they will realize now that it does not pay to make enemies of everyone."

"The Wokala will never learn a lesson," answered Wildoo. "They are always satisfied with themselves: and even though some may die, the others will forget all about it, once they have their shining white cloaks and can flock into the tree-tops again. But possibly they may not be so lucky—who can tell?" He also chuckled, looking as wise as an owl. But when Corridella asked him what he meant, he pretended to go to sleep: and Corridella, who knew better than to pester an Eagle with too many questions, said good evening and sailed homeward across the tree-tops.

Left to himself, Wildoo waited until no bird was in sight, and then flapped heavily away from his rocky shelf, and dived downward to the gully. It did not take him long to find the Wokala. They did not gleam with the whiteness of snow, for they were moulting and very shabby, and a few were dressed mainly in pin-feathers; but their voices were just as harsh as ever, and guided Wildoo to where they were huddling among some she-oak trees. Already a cold wind was whistling down between the hills, sighing and moaning in the she-oak branches. There is no tree in all Australia so mournful as the she-oak on a cold night, when each long needle seems to sing a separate little song of woe. Already the miserable Wokala were sorry that they had chosen to roost there.

Suddenly, great wings darkened the evening sky above them, and, looking up, they saw Wildoo. He perched on a limb of a dead gum-tree far overhead, and looked down at them, laughing. There seemed, to the shivering Wokala, something very terrible in the sound of his laughter.

"Kwah!" they whispered. "Wildoo has found us. Now he will be revenged." They knew they could not fly swiftly enough to escape him, and they began to creep downwards, hoping to hide among the bracken fern that clothed the gully. But Wildoo called to them, and, to their astonishment, his voice sounded friendly.

"Oh, Wokala!" he cried. "Are you very cold?"

"Ay, we are cold," said the Wokala, as well as they could, for their beaks were chattering with fear and shivering.

"No wonder, seeing how little you have on," said Wildoo. "A pity you did not get your new white feather cloaks ready earlier, instead of spending your time in annoying honest folk. Well, perhaps you will have more sense next year."

"Doubtless we shall, if we live," said the oldest Wokala. "But it seems likely that not many of us will live, for we are nearly frozen already."

"How distressing for you!" said Wildoo—"especially as it will be far colder before morning than it is now. These gullies are the chilliest places in the Bush on a frosty night."

The beaks of the Wokala chattered anew.

"We came for shelter," said the old Wokala miserably. "But you say truth, Wildoo: I think the Frost-Spirit has his home down here. Is it any warmer where you are?"

"Very little," said Wildoo—"and the wind is singing through these branches. But I know of a sheltered place, for all that."

"Kwah!" said the Wokala, all together. "A sheltered place! Oh, Wildoo, you are great and—and—and beautiful. Will you not tell us where it is?"

"Great and beautiful, am I?" said Wildoo, with a chuckle. "That is not the sort of thing you have been calling me all these months. However, it is lucky for you that I am also good-natured; I would not willingly see any of my people die of cold, not even the Wokala, who deserve little of anyone."

"Then you will tell us where is the sheltered place?" chattered the Wokala.

"Fly across to the Black Mountain," said Wildoo. "There is an ironstone wurley near the top—I will guide you to it, if you like. It is big enough for you all, and there is a fine heap of sticks on which to perch. The wind will not blow inside it, and the morning sun will shine right into it."

"It sounds too wonderful to be true," said the Wokala. "Is it dry, this ironstone wurley?"

"Dry as old bones," answered Wildoo. "Oh, you would be in luck to get there—you would forget all your troubles."

"One would think that impossible," shivered the old Wokala—he was very sorry for himself. "But if you will really guide us there, then be quick, Wildoo, or none of us will be able to fly at all."

"Very well," Wildoo answered. "I will go slowly, as I suppose you are all stiff. Follow me, and come down when you see me perch."

MARY GRANT BRUCE

He spread his great wings and looked down at them for a moment with a little smile; and if they had not been so eager and so cold they might have hesitated at the expression in his yellow eyes. But, as usual, the Wokala thought only of themselves, and as they had learned to believe that Wildoo was afraid of them, they never suspected that he might be leading them into a trap. They cried "Kwah! Kwah!" and rose into the air after him as soon as the flapping of the mighty wings told them that he had left the gum-tree. Even to fly slowly was difficult, so stiff with cold were they: but they all persevered, except one young hen—a pretty young thing, whose weary wings would not do their duty. She made a brave attempt to rise, but before the flight had cleared the big dead gum-tree she had to drop back—thankful to find a secure perch on a jutting limb.

"Ky!" she whimpered. "I can never fly all the way to the Black Mountain. I must die here."

She crept along the limb until she came to the trunk, and there luck awaited her. In the fork was an old 'possum-hole which had not been used for many seasons. It was dry and warm—sheltered from the bitter wind, and soft underfoot with rotting leaves, pleasant to the touch. The young Wokala hopped in thankfully, and it seemed the last touch to her wonderful good fortune that she immediately met a fine fat grub. She promptly ate it for her supper, tucked her head under her wing, nestled into the farthest corner, and went to sleep, remarking drowsily, "This is better than all Wildoo's ironstone wurleys!"

The other Wokala did not notice that the young hen had dropped back—or if they did they did not worry about her. Weary as they were, it took all their strength to keep Wildoo in sight, even though he kept his word and flew slowly. They were thankful when at length he sank lower and came to rest on a big boulder by the mouth of the cave near the mountain-top. The Wokala followed him in a straggling line, and perched on the shelf outside the cave.

"There you are," Wildoo said, nodding towards the yawning hole in the hillside. "That is your ironstone wurley, and I will promise you that you will find it dry and free from draughts."

"There is nothing living there?" asked the old Wokala, looking a little doubtfully at the cave.

"Nothing at all. All you will find there is a heap of dry sticks; you can perch there and keep each other warm. Stay there, if you like it well enough, until your new feather cloaks are ready—you are really scarcely fit for decent society now." Wildoo cast a half-contemptuous glance at the shivering, half-fledged birds, as they clustered on the rocky shelf. Then he flew off again into the gathering darkness.

"Whatever is Wildoo about?" asked Kellelek, the Cockatoo, of his hens. "He seems to be leading all the Wokala round the sky. A funny nurse he looked, and with a funny lot of chickens!"

"No wonder he waited for dusk before he would be seen with them," said one of his wives contemptuously. "I flew by their tree today, and really, they were a positive disgrace. And they always think themselves so smart!"

"Oh, they'll be smart enough again," said Kellelek, laughing. "Wait until they have their new feathers on, and you will be just as jealous of them as ever you were. There is no doubt that the Wokala are smart—that is, for people who prefer plain white. I like a good sulphur crest myself—but then, it's all a matter of opinion."

"Well, don't let the Wokala know that you admire them, or they will be worse than ever," said his wives, ruffling their feathers angrily.

Meanwhile, the Wokala had hesitated just for a moment before entering the cave. Then a fresh blast of cold wind swept across the face of the mountain, and they waited no longer, but fluttered in before it, in a hurrying, jostling flock. It was just as Wildoo had told them: warm and dry, and with a big heap of dry sticks in the middle—just the thing for them to perch on. They hopped up eagerly, huddling together for warmth, scrambling and fighting for the best places. Soon they were all comfortably settled, and at last warmth began to steal back into their shivering bodies.

"A good thing we made Wildoo afraid of us," said one sleepily. "Otherwise we should never have known of this splendid wurley." The others uttered drowsy murmurs of "Kwah!" as they drifted into slumber.

But far away on his mountain shelf Wildoo sat and waited, his yellow eyes wide and wakeful. The dusk deepened into night, and far off, from his perch on a tall stringy bark tree, old Wook-ook, the Mopoke, sent out his long cry, "Mo—poke! Mo—poke!" Presently came a dim radiance in the east and Wildoo stirred a little.

"Peera comes," he muttered.

Peera, the Moon, came up slowly, until all the Bush was flooded with her dim light, falling into shadow now and then, when dark clouds drifted across her face. Wildoo waited until she was above the tree-tops, with her beams falling upon the ironstone mountain. Then he took a fire-stick in his talons and flew swiftly away, never pausing until he alighted on the shelf before the cave.

He laid the fire-stick down and went softly to the dark opening, listening. There came only the sound of the breathing of the Wokala, with now and then a muffled caw as one dreamed, perhaps, of cold and hunger. As his eyes grew accustomed to the light, Wildoo could see them—a huddled white mass upon the heap of sticks. That was all he wanted, and he went back swiftly for his fire-stick, and with it went into the cave. Very softly he slipped it into the dry heart of the heap of sticks below the sleeping Wokala. He waited until little smoke-wreaths began to curl up, and a faint glow came from within the heap.

"Now you will be warm enough, my friends!" he muttered. He hurried out of the cave, and flew slowly to the nearest tree, on the hill opposite the Black Mountain. There he perched and waited. Very soon all the dark mouth of the cave was filled with glowing radiance, and clouds of smoke came billowing out and rolled down the hill. Then came loud and terrified cawing, and Wildoo thought he could see dark forms fluttering out through the smoke. His yellow eyes gleamed at the sight. And then clouds came suddenly across the face of the Moon, and a fierce wind blew, with driving rain that beat into the mouth of the cave. It blotted out the glow, and the wind carried away the cries. When all was quiet Wildoo flapped off to his nest.

He was back next morning on the boulder outside the cave, and with him all the birds of the Bush, whom he had collected as he came, saying to them, "Come and see what happens to those who insult Wildoo." The black mouth of the ironstone cave looked grim and forbidding, and, peering in, the birds could see the charred ends of the dry sticks, scattered on the floor round a heap of ashes. Then, from the inner recesses of the cave came a strange procession, and at the sight the Kooka burra burst into a peal of laughter. For it was the Wokala.

They came slowly—but where were their white feathers, of which they had been so proud? All were gone, singed off close to their bodies; and their bodies were blackened with smoke. Queer, naked birds they looked, creeping out into the sunshine, and there was no pride left in them. They looked up and saw Wildoo and the laughing birds of all the Bush; and with a loud miserable cawing they fled back into the cave.

No one saw the Wokala again for a time. But after a long while they came out again, this time with all their feathers fully grown. No longer, however, were they white—the whitest of all birds. Their new feathers were a glossy black!

They looked at each other for a moment with a kind of horror. Then they rose into the air with a swift beating of their jet-black wings, and, calling "Kwah! Kwah!" they fled across the sky. And as they flew another cawing was heard, and a white bird rose and flew to meet them—the Wokala hen who had been left behind, and who had taken refuge in the 'possum-hole. She was now the only white Wokala left in all the world. They met in mid-air, and at sight of the strange black birds with the familiar voices the white Wokala uttered a scream and fled away, never to be seen again.

Since then, always the Crows have been black. They found their old impudence again after a while, and became what they had been when they were white—always the nuisances of the Bush, vagabonds and robbers and bullies. But still the terror of the ironstone wurley is upon them, and they never venture into caves, but live in the big trees, where they can see far and wide, and where no creeping enemy can come upon them in the darkness. And Wildoo, the King of the Birds, never finds them near his nest, nor need he ever speak to them. One glance from him is enough for the Wokala: they would fly to the deepest recesses of the Bush rather than face the gleam of his yellow eyes.

MARY GRANT BRUCE

XII

Kur-bo-roo, the Bear

Chapter I

Kur-bo-roo was a little black boy baby. His father and mother had no other children, and so they were very proud of him, and he always had enough to eat. It is often very different when there are many hungry pickaninnies to be fed—especially in dry seasons, when roots and yams and berries are hard to find, and a black mother's task of filling her dilly-bag becomes more difficult every day. Then it may happen that the children are quite often hungry, and their ribs show plainly through their black skins: and they learn to pick up all kinds of odd food that white children would consider horrible—insects, grubs, and moths, and queer fungi, which may sometimes give them bad pains—although it is not an easy thing to give a black child indigestion.

But Kur-bo-roo had not known any hard times. He was born a cheerful, round baby, quite light in colour at first; and as he darkened he became rounder and jollier. His hair curled in tight little rings all over his head, and his nose was beautifully flat—so flat that his mother did not need to press it down to make him good-looking, as most of the black mothers do to their babies. He was very strong, too, with a straight little back and well-muscled limbs; and when his teeth came they could crunch up bones quite easily, or even the hard nardoo berries. His mother thought he was the most beautiful pickaninny that was ever born, which is an idea all mothers have about their babies. But Kur-bo-roo's mother *knew* that she was right.

He had so many good things to eat that he grew fatter and fatter. His father brought home game—wallaby, wombat, iguana, lace-lizards, porcupines, bandicoots, opossums; and though it was polite to give away a good deal to his wife's father, there was always plenty for little Kur-bo-roo. Then delicious bits of snake came his way, and long white tree-grubs, as well as all the native fruits and berries that the black women find; and he had plenty of creek water to drink. So long as you give a wild blackfellow good water he will always manage to forage for food.

Kur-bo-roo did not have to forage. It interested his father and mother tremendously to do all that they could for him, and watch him grow. As soon as he could toddle about, his father made him tiny throwing-sticks and a boomerang, and tried to teach him to throw them; and his mother, squatting in the shade of the wurley, would laugh to see the baby thing struggling with the weapons of a man. And, while she laughed, she was prouder than ever. She used to rub his limbs to make them supple and strong. He did not wear any clothes at all, so that she was never worried about keeping his wardrobe in order. Instead, she was able to give all her time to making him into what she thought to be the best possible kind of boy. And, however that may have been, it is quite certain that there never was a happier pickaninny.

It was when Kur-bo-roo was nearly six years old that the evil spirit of Trouble came to him.

Sickness fell upon the tribe. No one knew how it came, and the medicine-men could not drive it away. First of all, the people had terrible headaches, and the Meki-gar, or doctor, used to treat them in the usual manner—he would dig out a round sod of earth and, making the patient lie down with his head in the hole, would put the sod on his head, and stand on it, or sit on it, to squeeze out the pain. If this were not successful, he would tie a cord tightly round the patient's head, and cut him with a sharp shell or flint, beating his head with a little stick to make the blood flow freely. These excellent measures had in the past cured many severe headaches. But they could not cure the sickness now.

So the Meki-gar had the patient carried out of the camp. The bearers carried him slowly, singing a mournful chant; and behind them came all the sick man's friends, sweeping the ground with boughs, to sweep away the bad power that had caused the disease. This bad power was, the Meki-gar said, the work of a terrible being called Bori. But, whether it was Bori's fault, or whether the tribe had simply brought sickness on themselves by allowing the camp to become very dirty, the Meki-gar could not drive away the sickness. It grew worse and worse, and people died every day.

Kur-bo-roo was only a little lad, but he was unhappy and frightened, although he did not understand at all. The air was always full of the sound of the groaning and crying of those people who were ill, and of lamenting and mourning for the dead. Everybody was terribly afraid. The blacks believed that their bad spirits were angry with them, and that nothing could do them any good; and so, many died from sheer

MARY GRANT BRUCE

fright, thinking that once they were taken ill they were doomed, and that it was no good to make a fight against the mysterious enemy. That was stupid, but they did not know any better.

Then there came a heavy rain, and after it was over, and the sun had come out to smile upon a fresh, clean world, the sickness began to get better and pass away. But just at the last, it came to the wurley where Kur-bo-roo lived with his father and mother.

Kur-bo-roo could not understand why his parents could not get up and go to find food. They lay in the wurley together, shivering under all the 'possum rugs and talking quickly in queer, high voices that he could not make out at all. They called often for water, and he brought it to them in his little tarnuk, or drinking-vessel, going backwards and forwards to the creek, and up and down its banks, until his little legs were very tired. Long after he was tired he kept on going for water. Then there came a time when they could not lift the tarnuk, and he tried to hold it to their lips, so that they could drink; but he was not very successful, and much of the water was spilt. You see, he was only a very little, afraid boy.

He woke up one morning, cold and hungry. There was no more food in the wurley, and no voices: only a great silence. He crept under the 'possum rug to his father and mother, but they were quite still, and when he called to them, they did not answer. He rubbed their cold faces with a shaking little hand, but no warmth came to them. Then he broke into loud, frightened crying, like any other lonely little boy.

Presently some of the blacks came to the wurley and pointed at the quiet bodies under the 'possum rug, and jabbered very hard, beckoning to others to come. Kur-bo-roo heard them say "tumble-down" a great many times, and he knew that it meant "dead"; but he did not know that his father and mother would never speak to him anymore. Only when an old woman picked him up and carried him away he understood that a terrible thing had happened to him, and he cried more bitterly than ever, calling to his mother. She had always run to him when he called. But now she did not come.

Chapter II

AFTER THAT, HARD TIMES CAME upon little Kur-bo-roo. There were none of his own family left, for the sickness had taken them all. His father and mother had been the last to die, and that made the blacks think that very probably Bori, the Evil Spirit, had been especially angry with Kur-bo-roo's family, because so many of them had died and the last terrible blow of the disease had fallen on their wurley. Indeed, for awhile they argued as to whether it would not be better to kill Kur-bo-roo too, so that so troublesome a family should be quite stamped out, with no further chance of annoying Bori and bringing trouble upon the tribe. They did not spare him out of any idea of pity; but because so many men and boys had died that the tribe had become seriously weakened, and it seemed foolish to kill a strong and healthy fellow like Kur-bo-roo. It was very important for a tribe to keep up its fighting strength, for there was always a chance that another band of blacks might come upon them and want to fight: in which case the weaker tribe might be swallowed up. So boy babies were thought a good deal of, and for that reason the blacks did not make an end of little Kur-bo-roo.

But he had a very bad time, for all that. No one wanted him. He was nobody's boy; and that hurts just the same whether a boy be black or white. Never was there so lonely a little fellow. The other children were half afraid of him, because the fear of Bori's anger yet hung about him; they would not let him join in their games, and took a savage delight in hunting him away from their wurleys. Another black family had taken possession of his father's wurley, and no home was left to him. He used to wander about miserably, often sleeping in the open air, curled up in the shadow of a bush, or in a hollow tree-stump. If it were cold or wet, he would creep noiselessly into a hut when he thought everyone would be asleep—and quite often he was kicked out again.

He was always hungry now. His father and mother had taken such care of him, and had loved so much to keep him fed, that he had never learned how to find food for himself. He would wander about in the Bush, looking for such things as his mother had brought him, but he knew so little that often he ate quite the wrong things, which made him very sick. He learned a good deal about food in that way, but the learning was not pleasant work.

It was a bad year for food. Dry weather had come, and game was scarce; it was hard for the fighting-men to bring home enough for their own children, without having to provide for a hungry boy of six who belonged to nobody. Kur-bo-roo used to hang about the cooking-places in the hope of having scraps of food thrown to him, but not many came his way. When so many were hungry the food was quickly eaten up. Sometimes a woman, pitying the shrinking little lad, would hastily toss him a bone or a fragment of meat; and though you would not have cared for the way it was cooked, Kur-bo-roo thought that these morsels were the most delicious he had ever tasted.

You see, a wild blackfellow has not much to think about except food. He has no schools, no daily papers, no market days, or picture shows, or telephones. The wild Bush is his, and all he asks or expects of it is that it shall supply him with food. He knows that it means strength to him, and that strength means happiness, as a rule, when all that he has depends upon his own ability to keep it for himself. He does not reason things that way, for the blackfellow is simple, but he just eats as much as he can whenever he can get it, and that seems to agree with him excellently. That was the principle on which Kur-bo-roo had been brought up, and it had made him the round, black, shiny baby that he had been until his parents died.

He was not nearly so round and shiny now. His little body was thin and hard, and he did not look so strong as before. It was not altogether lack of food that had weakened him—the want of happiness had a great deal to do with it.

He had found out that the tribe did not like him. Not only was he nobody's boy, but he was the object of a kind of distrust that he could feel without at all understanding it; and he had learnt to shrink and cringe from blows and bitter words. Once he had found a lace-lizard asleep on a rock, and, grasping his tiny waddy, had stolen up to it very carefully, all the instinct of the hunter blazing in his dark, sad eyes. The lizard, when it woke, was quick, but Kur-bo-roo was quicker—the stick came down with all the force of his arm, and he carried off his prey in triumph, meaning to ask a woman who had sometimes been kind to him if she would cook it for him. But just outside the camp three big boys had come upon him as he was carrying his prey, and that had been the last that Kur-bo-roo had seen of his lizard. He had fought for it like a little tiger—quite hopelessly, of course, but to fight had been a kind of dismal satisfaction to him, even though he was badly beaten in addition to losing his dinner; and that was specially unfortunate, for blacks think lizard a very great delicacy indeed. The boys ran off with it, jeering at the sobbing little figure on the ground; and they called him names that, even in his angry soreness, made him think. They said something to do with an evil spirit—he pondered over it, creeping into a clump of bushes. Why should they call him that?

Blacks always want a reason for any happening. Sometimes they are satisfied with very foolish reasons; but they must have something to explain occurrences, especially if they are unpleasant ones. The sickness that had fallen on their tribe they put down to Bori, as the medicine-man told them; but when the sickness had gone, it seemed only reasonable to believe that Bori was satisfied and would leave them alone for awhile. So they could not understand why misfortune should still pursue them. Another tribe had stolen part of their country, and they had been too weakened by the sickness to fight for it; and now had come the drought, making food harder than ever to obtain, and causing some of the babies to fall sick and die. They turned to the magic-men or sorcerers for explanation, and these clever people performed a great many extraordinary tricks to make things better. Then, as they were really hard up for some object on which to throw the blame of their failure, it occurred to them to turn suspicion towards little Kur-bo-roo.

Kur-bo-roo went on with his unhappy little life, quite ignorant of the storms gathering round his woolly head. No one was ever kind to him, and he could scarcely distinguish one day from another; although he gathered a vague idea that in some way they were linking his name with the Evil Spirit, he did not understand what that meant. He kept on hunting round for food and water, and dodging blows and angry faces. If he had guessed that the magic-men were busily persuading the people that his family and he were the cause of the terrible year through which they had passed, he might have been more uneasy; but, in any case, he was only a very little boy, and perhaps he would not have understood. He had enough troubles to think of without looking out for more.

Chapter III

THEN THE WORST PART OF the drought happened, for the creek began to run dry.

Day after day it ran a little more slowly, and the deep holes at the bends shrank and dwindled away. The fish disappeared completely, having swum down-stream to where deeper waters awaited them; and so another source of food was lost to the tribe. There only remained the black mud-eels, and soon it was hard to find any of these, try as they might. That was bad, but it was nothing in comparison to the loss of the water supply. Without the creek, the tribe could not exist, for the only other drinking-places in their country were swamps and morasses, and these, too, were dried up and useless. So the magic-men and head-men became very anxious, and many were the black glances cast upon the unconscious Kur-bo-roo as he slunk round the camp or hunted for food in the scrub. Then the head-men issued a command that no one should drink from the creek itself, lest the little water remaining should be stirred up and made muddy, or lest anyone should drink too much. Instead of going to the creek to drink, they were permitted to fill their tarnuks, or drinking-vessels, each morning; and then no one was allowed to approach the creek again that day. So in the mornings a long procession of women went down to the bank, where a head-man watched them fill the tarnuks, remaining until the last had hurried away, very much afraid of his fierce eyes.

But the new law fell very heavily on Kur-bo-roo, for he had now no tarnuk. The little one made for him by his father long ago had disappeared when he lost everything, and since then he had always been accustomed to drink at the creek. Now, however, he could not do so, and no one would give him a tarnuk, or let him drink from theirs. He would have stolen it very readily, for he was now not at all a well-brought-up little boy, but the tarnuks were hung far beyond his reach.

Of course, the magic-men knew how the new law would affect the little fellow. They knew that now it would be impossible for Kur-bo-roo to drink, and after a little he would "tumble-down" and be dead; and then, perhaps, the Evil Spirit would be satisfied, and go away from the tribe. They watched him carefully, and were glad that he became weak and wretched. They had uttered such savage penalties against drinking from the creek that it never occurred to them that he would dare to disobey. But sometimes in the darkness Kur-bo-roo used to creep down for a drink, being, indeed, as desperate as a boy can be, and quite sure that unless he went he must die; and he had become so stealthy in his movements that he was never caught. It did not satisfy his thirst, of course, for it was the hottest part of the summer, and all the blacks were accustomed to drinking a great deal: still, it was something. At least, it kept him alive.

Then, one morning, came news of a number of kangaroo feeding two miles away by the creek, and all the camp fell into a state of tremendous excitement at the very idea of such a chance of food. All the men and big boys dashed off at once, and presently the women made up their minds that they would follow them, as it was not at all unlikely that if the men had good luck in their hunt they might immediately sit down and eat a great portion of the game they had killed—in which case there was only a poor look-out for those left in camp. So they gathered up their dilly-bags and sticks, slung the babies on their backs, and ran off into the Bush after the men, leaving the camp deserted.

Now, it chanced that Kur-bo-roo knew nothing of all this. He had not spent the night in camp, because, on the evening before, he had been savagely beaten by two big boys, who had caught him alone in the scrub, and when they had finished with him he was too sick and sore to crawl back to the wurleys. He had crept under a bush, and slept there uneasily, for the pain of his bruises kept waking him up. The sun was quite high in the sky before he made up his mind to go back to the camp, in the faint hope that some one would give him food. So he limped slowly through the Bush, wincing when the harsh boughs rubbed against his sore limbs.

He stopped at the edge of the camp and rubbed his fists into his eyes, blinking in surprise. No one was in sight; instead of the hum and bustle of the camp, the men sitting about carving their spears and throwing-sticks, the women chattering round the wurleys, the babies rolling on the ground and playing with the dogs, there was only desolation and silence. He approached one hut after another, and poked in a timid head, but he saw no one, and the stillness seemed almost terrible to him. Then, in a corner of one wurley he saw a rush-basket, and from it came a smell that would have been disgusting to anyone but a black, but was pure delight to Kur-bo-roo. His fear vanished as he seized upon the food and ate it ravenously.

He came out presently, his thin little body not nearly so hollow as before, and looked about him. The food had made him feel better, but he was terribly thirsty. And then he saw, with a little glad shout, that all about the camp were drinking-vessels, brimming with water—put down wherever their owners had happened to be when they had rushed away to the hunt. Kur-bo-roo did not know anything about that, of course; he only knew that here was water enough to make him forget that he had ever been thirsty. He ran eagerly to the nearest tarnuk and drank and drank until he could drink no more.

And with that drink, so the blacks say, a great change came upon little Kur-bo-roo.

Kur-bo-roo put down the tarnuk and stood upright, throwing his head back in sheer bodily happiness at once more having had enough to eat and drink. All his bruises and soreness had suddenly gone; he was no longer tired and lonely and unhappy, but strong and well and glad. How wonderfully strong he felt! A new feeling ran through all his body.

"I am stronger than anybody ever was before!" he said aloud. And he believed that it was true.

He glanced round the deserted camp. It was quiet now, but he felt sure that soon the blacks would come hurrying back. Perhaps they would be there in a moment: Kur-bo-roo listened, half dreading to hear the quick pad-pad of bare feet over the hard, baked ground. No sound came. But he knew that they would return: and then, what would await him?

His new strength seemed to burn him. He stretched his arms out, wondering at their hard muscles, although he felt that the drink had been Magic, and so he need not wonder at anything at all. Some good Spirit, perhaps sorry for lonely little boys, had evidently come to help him. Fear suddenly left him altogether, and with its going came a mighty desire for revenge. He did not know what he was going to do, but the new power that was in him urged him on.

A little tree grew in front of him. He began to gather up all the drinking-vessels, and, one by one, to hang them upon the boughs. There were very many, and it took a long time, but at last the task was completed, and not a tarnuk was left in the camp. He looked in the wurleys, and found many empty vessels, and these also he hung up in the tree. Then he took the biggest tarnuk of all, and a little tarnuk, and went down to the creek: and with the little tarnuk he filled the big one, dipping up all the water from the creek, until there was none left. There was much water, yet still the big tarnuk held it all, and only the mud of the creek-bed remained where the stream had been rippling past. Even as he looked, that grew dry and hard. Then Kur-bo-roo turned and carried his burden up the bank to his tree, and from the big tarnuk he filled all the empty ones. They held a great deal, and yet the big tarnuk remained quite full. For now there was Magic in everything that Kur-bo-roo touched.

He climbed up into the little tree and seated himself comfortably in a fork, where he could see everything, and yet lean back comfortably. A quiver ran through the tree, as if something far underground had shaken it; and suddenly it began to grow. It grew and grew, spreading wide arms to the sky, until it was as large as very many big trees all put together: and its trunk was tall and straight and very smooth. All the time, Kur-bo-roo sat in the fork and smiled.

When the tree had finished growing, he heard a sound of voices far below him, and, looking down, he saw the tribe hurrying back through the scrub to their camp. Their hunt had been unsuccessful, for all the kangaroo had got away into the country of another tribe, where they dared not follow: so they were returning, hungry and thirsty, and in a very bad temper, for they had not found any water in the places where they had been. They came angrily back to the camp, and from his seat in the fork of the great tree Kur-bo-roo looked down at them and smiled.

The blacks were far too thirsty to look up at any tree. They hurried to the wurleys. Then the first said, "Where is my tarnuk?" and another said, "Wah! my tarnuk has gone!" and a third, "Who has taken all our tarnuks?" They became very angry, and beat their wives because they could find no drinking-vessels and no water: then, becoming desperate because of their thirst, they hurried to the creek. And lo! the creek was dry! They came back from the creek, jabbering and afraid, believing that the Evil Spirits had done this wonderful thing. Presently one saw the big tree, and cried out in astonishment.

"Ky! What tree is that?" he exclaimed.

They gathered round, staring in amazement at the huge tree: and so they saw all their tarnuks hanging in its branches, and little Kur-bo-roo sitting smiling in the fork.

"Wah! is that you?" they called. "Have you any water?"

"Yes, here am I, and I have plenty of water," said Kur-bo-roo. "But I will not give you one drop, because you would give me none, although I died of thirst."

Some threatened him, and some begged of him, and the women and children wailed round the base of the tree. But Kur-bo-roo smiled down at them, and took no heed of all their anger and their crying. Then a couple of young men took their tomahawks of stone and began to climb the tree, although they were afraid, because it was so big. Still, thirst drove them, and so they came up the tree, cutting notches for their fingers and toes in the smooth trunk, and coming wonderfully quickly. But Kur-bo-roo laughed, and let fall a little water on them from a tarnuk; and as soon as the water touched them, they fell to the ground and were killed.

Again and again other men tried to climb the tree, becoming desperate with their own thirst and the crying of the women and children; but always they met the same fate. Always Kur-bo-roo smiled, and splashed a few drops of water upon them: only a drop on each of them, but as the drops touched them their hold loosened, the grip of their toes relaxed, and they fell from the great height, to meet their death on the ground below. So it went on until nearly all the men of the tribe were gone: and Kur-bo-roo sat in the fork of the tree and smiled.

And it still went on, all through the moonlit night. But in the dawn two men came back from hunting: Ta-jerr and Tarrn-nin, the sons of Pund-jel, Maker of Men. They were very cunning, as well as being very brave, and after they had taken counsel together, they began to climb the tree. But they did not climb as the other men had done, straight up the long line of the smooth trunk. Instead, they climbed round and round, as the clematis creeps when it throws its tendrils about a branch.

Kur-bo-rop laughed, just as he had laughed at the others, and waited until they had ascended to a great height. Then he took water, and let it fall—but the men were no longer in the same place, but on the other side, climbing round and round, and he missed them. Again and again he ran to get more, and poured it down; they were very quick, circling about the trunk, and always managed to escape the falling drops. They came to the place where the trunk forked, and swung themselves into the high boughs.

Then little Kur-bo-roo began to cry in a terrified voice. But they seized him, not heeding, and beat him until all his bones were broken, and then threw him down. The other blacks uttered a great shout of triumph, and ran to kill him.

But the Magic that had helped him came to the aid of little Kur-bo-roo once more, and so he did not die. Suddenly, just as the angry blacks were upon him, with uplifted waddies and threatening faces, he changed under their gaze; and where there had been a little black boy there lay for a moment a Native Bear, his grey fur bristling, and fear filling his soft eyes. Then, very swiftly, he gathered himself up and ran up a tree, until he was out of sight among the branches.

Just then the blacks were too thirsty to pursue him. Overhead, Ta-jerr and Tarrn-nin were cutting at the branches of the great tree that held the tarnuks; and all the water came out and flowed back to the creek, and again the creek became wide and clear, running swiftly in its bed so that there was drink for all. Then Ta-jerr and Tarrn-nin came down to the ground, and the tribe hailed them as heroes. But when they looked for little Kur-bo-roo, the Native Bear, he had fled into another tree, and had disappeared.

From that time, the Native Bears became food for the black people. But it is law that they must not break their bones when they kill them, nor must they take off their skin before they cook them. So they take them carefully, hitting them on the head; and they cook them by roasting them whole in an oven of stones, sunk in the ground. If the law were broken, Kur-bo-roo would again become powerful, the magic-men say; and the first thing he would do would be to dry up all the creeks.

Now, Kur-bo-roo lives near the creeks and water holes, so that if the people broke the law he might at once carry away the water. He is not very wise, because he was only quite a little boy before he became a Native Bear, and so had not much time to gain wisdom: but he is soft, and fat, and gentle, unless you interfere with him when he wants to climb a tree, and then he can scratch very hard with his sharp claws. All he can do is to climb, and he does not see very well in the daytime: therefore, he thinks that whatever he meets is a tree, and at once he tries to climb it. If the blacks throw things at him when he is sitting in the fork of a tree, he blinks down at them, and sometimes you might think he smiles. But if they climb his tree and come near to knock him down, he cries always, very terribly—just as he cried long ago, when he was Magic and Ta-jerr and Tarrn-nin climbed his great tree and threw him to the people far below.

XIII

WURIP, THE FIRE-BRINGER

Chapter I

ONCE THERE WAS A TIME when the blacks had no fire. They had not learned the way to make it by rubbing two sticks together; or if they had once known the way, they had forgotten it. And they were very miserable, for it was often cold and wintry, and they had no fire to warm them, nor any way of cooking food.

Fire had been theirs once. But there came two women upon the Earth; strange women, speaking in unknown tongues, with great eyes in which there was no fear. They did not love the blacks. They lived in their camps for a time, and built for themselves a wurley, coming and going as they pleased; but always there was hatred in their wild eyes, and the blacks feared them exceedingly. Because they feared them, although they hated them, they gave them food, and the women cooked it for themselves, for at that time the fire blossomed at the door of every hut.

But one day, the blacks awoke to find the women gone. They had gone in the night, silently, and with them they took all the fire that the blacks had. There was not even a coal left to start the hearth-blaze for the shivering people.

The fighting-men made haste to arm themselves, and started in pursuit of the women. They travelled through swamps and morasses, across boggy lands and creeks fringed with reeds and sedges; all the time seeing nothing of the women, but knowing that they were on the right track, by the faint smell of fire that still hung in the air. "They have gone this way, carrying Fire!" they said. "Soon we shall overtake them." And they pressed on, going faster and faster as the smell of burning wood became stronger and stronger.

At last they came out upon a little open space, and, looking across it, they saw a new wurley made of bushes interlaced with reeds. In front of it smoke curled up lazily, and they caught the gleam of red coals, and yellow flame. The two women sat by the fire, motionless. The fighting-men broke into a run, shouting: "Now we will make an end of these women!" they cried fiercely to each other, as they ran, gripping their spears and throwing-sticks.

The women sat by the fire taking no heed. So little did they seem to notice the running warriors that it seemed that they did not see them; or, if they did see them, they cared no more than for a line of black swans flying westward into the sunset. One stirred the fire gently, and laid across the red embers a dried stick of she-oak. The other weaved a mat of rushes in a curious device of green and white; and as she twisted them in and out, she smiled. Even when the long shout of the fighting-men sent its echoes rolling round the sky, they did not look up. The glow of the flames shone reflected deep in their eyes.

So the fighting-men came on, grim and relentless, burning with the anger of all their long chase and the hot desire for revenge. They tightened their grip on their waddies, since there was nothing to be gained by risking a throwing-stick or a spear when the enemy to be slain was only two women, weak and unarmed. For such defenceless creatures, a blow with a waddy would be sufficient. But, half a spear's cast from the wurley, something they could not see brought them to a sudden, gasping halt. It was as though a wall were there, soft and invisible, but yet a wall. They could not touch it to climb over it, neither could they force their way through. They struck at it, and it was as if their sticks struck the empty air. There was nothing to see but the wurley, and the fire, and the quiet women, and the air was clear and bright. But no step farther could they advance.

They circled about the camp, trying at every step to get nearer to the wurley. It was all to no purpose: always the wall met them, though they could not see it. So they came back to the point whence they had started, breathless, angry, and a little afraid. They were brave men, and used to battle, but it is easier to fight a visible enemy than one that lurks, unseen, in the air. It was Magic, and they knew it. Still, their anger burned furiously within them, and one lifted a spear tipped with poisoned bone, and flung it at the women. To see him lift his hand was enough for the band. A storm of spears went hurtling through the air.

For a few yards the spears flew straight and true. But then they stopped suddenly in mid-flight, as though an unseen wall had met them. For a moment they seemed to hang in the air, then they fell in a jangling heap among the tussocks. And beyond them, while the terrified warriors shrank together, gesticulating and trembling, the women laid more sticks upon the fire, and smiled.

MARY GRANT BRUCE

The fighting-men were cunning, and they did not give in easily. Not only were they smarting with the fury of defeat, but the tale was not one they wished to carry back to the tribe, lest they should become a laughing-stock even to the women and young boys. So they drew off, thinking under cover of night to renew the attack in the hope that when the women slept their Magic would also sleep. So, when darkness had fallen, they crept up again, on noiseless feet. But the invisible wall was there, and they could find no gap in its circle; while, all the time, the fire burned redly before the wurley, and the women sat by it, feeding it, and weaving their mats of white and green.

At length the warriors became weak for want of food, and weary of the useless struggle; and so they gave up the fight and slowly made their way back, across swamp-land and morass, to the tribe that waited for them, shivering and fireless, in the shadow of the hills.

Great and bitter were the lamentations at the news of their defeat. They had been eagerly watched for; and when they came slowly back to the camp, trailing their spears, a long cry of angry disappointment rent the air. It was difficult to believe their story. Who could imagine a wall, strong enough to stop warriors, yet that could not be seen? So they found themselves coldly looked upon, and their wives said unpleasant things to them in their wurleys that night. Quite a number of wives had sore heads next morning—since it was easier to deal with a talkative wife by means of a waddy than by argument. But the wives had the last word, for all that, and the small boys of the tribe used to call jeering words at the disgraced warriors, from the safe concealment of a clump of dogwood, or fern. Meanwhile, there was no cooked food. The tribe was very far from being happy.

Then a band of young men, who were not picked warriors, but were anxious to distinguish themselves, made up their minds that they would go forth to find the Fire-Women and slay them, and bring back Fire to the tribe. They were very young men, and so they were confident that they could succeed where the warriors had failed; and for at least a week before they started they went about the camp telling everyone how they meant to do it. When they were not doing this, or singing songs about the great deeds they meant to perform—and very queer songs they were—they were polishing their weapons and making new ones, and talking together, at a great rate, of their secret plans. When they were ready, at last, they painted themselves with as much pipe-clay as they were allowed to use, and gathered together to start.

"When we have killed the Fire-Women," they said to the tribe, "some of us will turn homewards and wait here and there along the way. Then the others will run with the fire-stick, and as they grow tired those that have gone ahead will take it and run very swiftly back to you. In three days the tribe will be cooking food with the fire which we shall bring. Then we shall get married and have wurleys and fires of our own."

All the blacks listened gravely, except the fighting-men who had not brought back anything at all. These men laughed a little, but no one took any notice of their laughter, because they had failed, and it is the way of the world not to think well of failures. The girls thought the band of young warriors wonderfully noble, and smiled upon them a great deal as they marched out of the camp. Of course, the boys were much too proud to smile back again—but then, the girls did not expect them to, and were quite content to do all the smiling. So the little band marched off with a great flourish, and the Bush swallowed them up.

"May they come back soon!" said one girl, as she and her companions dug for yams next day.

"Ay!" said the others. "We are weary of eating things which are not cooked."

"I am weary of being cold," said one. "There is but one 'possum rug in our wurley, and my father takes it always."

"There will be great feasting and joy when they bring Fire back," said another. "Perhaps some of us will be married, too." And they laughed and made fun of each other, after the fashion of girls of any colour.

But the three days had not past when the young men returned: and when they came, they sneaked back quietly into the camp and tried to look as if they had not gone at all. They had washed the pipe-clay from their bodies, and were all quite anxious to work very hard and make themselves exceedingly useful to the older men; nor were they at all anxious to talk. They gave severe blows to the young boys who clustered round them, clamouring for news, and told them to go and play. But when they were summoned before the leaders, they hung their heads and told the same story as the warriors. They had seen the Fire-Women, they said, and they still sat before their wurley and fed the fire; but the young men could not come near them, nor could any of their weapons reach them. And when they were wearied with much throwing, and their arms had grown stiff and sore, a great fear came suddenly upon them, and they turned and fled homeward through the scrub, never stopping until they came upon the huts they knew. Now they were very much ashamed, and the girls mocked at them, but the warriors shook their heads understandingly.

"To fight is no good," they said. "Unless the magic-men can tell us how to beat down the magic wall and conquer the Fire-Women, the tribe will go for ever without Fire. We are wonderfully brave, but we cannot fight witchcraft. Let the magic-men undertake the task, for indeed it is a thing beyond the power of simple men. But is it not for such matters that we keep the magic-men?"

Then all the tribe said, "Yes, that is what we have been thinking all along." And they looked expectantly at the magic-men, demanding that they should at once accomplish the business, without any further trouble. Everyone became quite pleased and hopeful, except the magic-men themselves—and *they* were in a very bad temper, because they did not like the task.

Still they held their heads high, and made little of the matter, because to do anything else would have been imprudent: and they looked as wise as possible—a thing they had trained themselves to do, whether they knew anything about a matter or not. All kinds of wise men can do this, and it is a very handy habit, because it makes people think them even wiser than they are. They went away by themselves, with dreadful threats of what might happen if the people came near them—not that there was any need for them to take such precautions, for the blacks were much too terrified by them to venture near when they were working any kind of Magic.

A great deal of what the blacks called Magic would seem very stupid to you if you watched it now; but they all believed in it firmly, and even those who knew that they deceived others still thought that Magic was a real thing, and that it could be practised upon them. The magic-men shut themselves up for a time; and then they told the men that they had made themselves into crows, and had flown over to watch what the Fire-Women were doing. As all the tribe believed that they could turn themselves into any animal they chose, and be invisible, nobody thought of doubting this. The magic-men then began to weave spells. They chopped the branches from a young she-oak tree, and cleared away grass and sticks in a circle round it. Then they sharpened the end of the trunk, and drew on the ground the figure of a woman, with the lopped tree growing out of her chest. Afterwards they rubbed themselves all over with charcoal and grease, and danced and sang songs round the tree for some days, expecting the Fire-Women to feel their Magic, so that they would have to rise from their camp and walk, as if in a sleep, to the place of the dance. But the women did not come, and so the magic-men told themselves that they were not yet strong enough. Meanwhile, the tribe clustered some distance off, very frightened and respectful, and also very cold.

The magic-men tried other plans, although they were much hampered because many of their spells needed the use of Fire, and there was none to be had. They tried to kill the women by pointing magic things in the direction of their camp, such as bones, and pieces of quartz-crystal, which were believed to be very deadly; and, going to their old wurley, they put sharp fragments of bone in any footprints they could find, thinking that the women would fall ill and become very lame, and so lose their power. But nothing happened. So they sent one of their number secretly through the Bush, and he returned to tell them that the women were well and unharmed, and that the invisible wall about their camp was just as strong as ever.

Then the magic-men knew that they could do no more. They told the people that the only spells that would conquer the Fire-Women were spells in which Fire formed a part; and until they could bring them Fire, they must not expect to be freed from the power of the women. The tribe did not like this, and much lamentation went up; but they were much too afraid of the magic-men to object openly to anything they did.

Chapter II

AT THIS TIME THERE LIVED in the tribe a man called Wurip.

He was not a lucky man. Once, in a big tribal fight, most of his relations had been killed; and when he was still quite a young man, his wife died of a mysterious sickness, before they had been married very long. Then, one night, he tripped and fell into a big fire, burning himself terribly. He got better, but his left arm and hand were quite twisted and withered, and were of very little use to him.

Had he been a different kind of man, it is not unlikely that he would have been killed by the tribe, for the blacks had no use for maimed or deformed persons. But Wurip was strong, apart from his twisted arm; and also he had a way of muttering to himself that rather frightened people. It was only a habit, but the blacks were always afraid of what they could not understand. So they left him alone.

He lived in a little wurley by himself, and though he was lonely, and would have liked to take another wife, he knew that no girl would want a man whose arm and hand were not like those of other men. So he did not try to get married, and gradually he became very solitary. He thought the other men disliked him, and he would go away by himself on hunting expeditions, and wander through the scrub alone. Although he was half a cripple, he soon learned to know the Bush more thoroughly than any man in the tribe, and he trained his shrivelled arm to do a great deal, although at first it had seemed that it must be useless for ever. The other blacks at first gave him nick-names about his arm, but he did not like them, and his eyes were so fierce that they did not let him hear them anymore, and to his face only called him by his own name, Wurip, which means "a little bird."

Now, Wurip loved his tribe. He had no special friends in it, which was partly his own fault, for he had grown very unsociable, but he was proud of the tribe itself, because it was brave and owned good country, and had been successful in many fights. It made him sore at heart to see it suffering from the want of Fire, and also it hurt his pride that it should have been beaten by women. So he made up his mind that he would try to recover Fire from the wicked Fire-Women. He thought about it for a long time, and laid his plans very carefully.

One day he left the camp, carrying no weapons, but only a single waddy. The other blacks said to him:

"Where are you going?"

Wurip said, "I go to try to get Fire back."

"You!" they said. "A little man, and crippled! That is very funny." And all the people laughed at him.

Wurip hesitated, and a gleam came into his eyes, so quick and fierce that those who had laughed shrank back. Then he turned on his heel and walked off into the scrub, and the blacks said, "Let him go. He is mad, and he will most likely be killed; and it really does not matter. He is not much use."

Into the wild Bush Wurip went, taking short noiseless strides. He was a little man, but he had the quick movements of many little men, and at all times he could move rapidly through the Bush, scarcely making a sound as he went.

He passed through the scrub, and came to boggy lands and morasses; his light feet carried him over swamps and across creeks fringed with reeds and sedges. Then he saw a light curl of smoke going lazily skywards, and at the sight his heart gave a leap, for it was long since he had seen Fire.

Until then he had travelled very quickly. But now he slackened his speed and went slowly across the plain towards the Fire-Women's camp. As he drew near he could see them, sitting in front of the wurley and weaving their rushes. They did not look up as he came, and he advanced so near them that he began to think that the magic wall could be there no longer. Just as he was wondering if this were indeed true, one of the Fire-Women glanced up and saw him; and almost immediately Wurip felt some invisible object blocking his way, and knew he could go no farther.

He stopped, and burst out laughing, and at the sound of his merriment the other Fire-Woman glanced up sharply from her weaving, and the first one paused, with a stick of she-oak wood in her hand, and looked at him in blank astonishment. So silent was the place that Wurip's shout of laughter echoed like a thunderclap. The Fire-Women looked at the little black figure standing among the harsh tussocks of swamp-grass, and he waved to them with his withered arm. But they took no further notice, going on scornfully with their work.

Wurip had expected nothing else, and he was not discouraged. He began collecting sticks and brushwood for a wurley, singing as he went about his work, in full view of the two women. He made no further attempt to get through the invisible wall. There was not much timber about, and to find suitable material for his wurley was a difficult task. He walked slowly, using his crippled arm very little, because he hoped that the women would be less careful about him if they regarded him as a one-armed man. Sometimes he felt that they were looking at him, and then he would work with particular awkwardness. Always, however, he sang, and went about with a merry countenance, as if he had not a single care in the world.

He built his wurley and went off into the swamp to hunt, returning with some lizards and grubs, and a duck that he had caught just as it settled on a sedgy pool. Standing a little way back from the wall, he called out and threw the duck towards the fire where the women sat. But it fell before it reached them, meeting the unseen obstacle.

"What a pity—it is for you!" called Wurip, slowly, so that they could hear easily. "It is a fat duck." And saying this he laughed again, and went into his wurley, where he ate his supper contentedly—although it was not cooked—and went to sleep.

　　　　　　　　　　　　　　　MARY GRANT BRUCE

In the morning, the women were sitting as before. But the duck had gone, and, looking closely across the little space, Wurip saw that there were feathers lying about near their fire. Also there was a pleasant smell of cooking in the air. This gladdened his heart, for it showed that the women did not mind making him useful, and that was exactly what he wanted.

So the days went by, and Wurip lived in his wurley, and the women in theirs. He never saw them away from it. Neither did he try anymore to go near it. From time to time he made them friendly signals, or called cheerful greetings to them, but that was all. Each day he went hunting, and good luck always attended him, because it was the time when waterfowl are plentiful, and as no others hunted there, the birds were not afraid. It was quite easy to fill the bag he had made out of rushes. And each evening he put the best of the game on a big stone some distance from his wurley, and in the morning it was always gone.

This went on for fourteen days. When he was not hunting, Wurip lay about his camp, always singing contentedly as he carved himself boomerangs or whittled heads for throwing-spears that he never used. Once he carved a bowl from a root that he found, and this also he put on the stone, for the Fire-Women, and they took it. He gathered bundles of the rushes that women of the tribes use in weaving, and left them too. So that he became very useful to them, although he had never heard their voices.

Then, after fourteen days, Wurip pretended that he had fallen sick. He did not go out hunting anymore, neither did he place offerings upon the big stone. In his wurley he had hidden sufficient food for himself to last him for several days, but he did not let the Fire-Women see him eating. Instead, he crawled out, dragging himself along the ground, and cried out, sorrowfully, waving his withered arm to them. He crawled back into his wurley and ate and slept; but they did not come, as he had hoped they would.

Next day he did not go out into the open at all. He kept close within his wurley, and all the exercise he took was to groan very mournfully. He groaned nearly all day, and by the time it was evening he was more tired than if he had hunted for three days. Because he was tired he ate nearly all that remained of his food, after which he felt discouraged, for he realized that it would soon be necessary to go out hunting again, and he wanted to seem ill. So he groaned more loudly than ever, and once or twice cried out as if in pain. Then he fell asleep.

The Fire-Women were fierce creatures, but still they were women. It troubled them that this crippled little blackfellow should be ill, too ill to bring them gifts or to busy himself, singing and laughing about his camp. To sit over a fire and weave mats of white and green may, in time, become dull; and it cheered the women to see Wurip and listen to his songs. When he did not appear they took counsel together, agreeing that so small a fellow, with a withered arm, could not be dangerous.

So, in the morning, Wurip heard steps, and opening his eyes, he saw one of the women entering his wurley. He almost jumped up; then, remembering, he groaned heavily, and looked at her with a stupid stare. She spoke to him, asking what was the matter, but he only moaned in answer. So she picked him up—it was not difficult, for she was very powerful, and Wurip was quite light—and carried him over to where her sister sat. There seemed to be no invisible wall now: the Fire-Woman walked to the fire, and put Wurip down before it. He nearly shouted, it was so long since he had been near a fire: but, luckily, he remembered to turn the shout into a groan.

For some days Wurip pretended to be very ill, and the Fire-Women nursed him—not in the harsh fashion of the medicine-men, but in gentler manner, feeding him, and giving him a comfortable bed to lie on. Wurip was only too glad to lie still and be fed, and it was not hard for him to pretend to be ill, because, being black, he was not required to look pale. Moreover, to taste cooked food once more nearly made him weep with joy. He was very grateful to the Fire-Women, and told them that he was an outcast from the tribe, because of his crippled arm, and he begged that, when he grew better, they would allow him to serve them.

The Fire-Women were not sorry to have a servant. Getting food and firewood was not very entertaining for them, and the gathering of rushes was a long and laborious task, which they hated. There could, they thought, be no risk in taking so harmless a person as Wurip to work for them. Still, they were stern with him. They told him that when he was well he must live in his own wurley and only come near theirs when it was necessary. Also, they assured him that if he were unfaithful to them their Magic would strike him dead immediately. This made Wurip think very hard, for he did not want to meet such an unpleasant fate, although he was quite determined to take Fire back to his tribe.

He showed great horror at the idea of being unfaithful, and when he thought it was prudent to get better he recovered his strength—not

MARY GRANT BRUCE

too quickly, for it was very pleasant to be nursed—and then began his duties. The Fire-Women found him an excellent servant. He was always at hand when he was wanted, and he did his work well. There was plenty of food at all times, and very long fine rushes that he found when he was hunting far from the camp. Wood he brought also, but the Fire-Women would never allow him to go near the fire. He laid the sticks at a little distance away: and they tended the fire and cooked the food, giving him a share. Altogether, they were very happy and comfortable, and if he had been able to forget the shivering tribe, Wurip would have been content. Although he was only a servant, he was less lonely than he had been in the company of the other blacks. The Fire-Women were stern with him, but they never made him remember that his arm was crippled—and when he had been with the tribe he could not forget for an instant that he was different to the others.

Sometimes in the evenings, as he lay in his wurley, the thought came to him that it would be better to forget the tribe and stay with the Fire-Women. After all, they were good to him in their fierce fashion, and he remembered that he had very little to look forward to, in returning to the big camp. Even if he took back the long-lost Fire, they might be grateful to him for a little while, but he would never be as the other men were.

And then Memory would come to him, bringing back pictures of the tribe, half starved and shivering; of the little children who were dying for want of proper food and warmth, and of the cold hearth-stones of his people. However they might treat him, he could not forget that they were his own people. He knew that he must go back to them.

Chapter III

WURIP LAY ON HIS BACK in the shade of a golden wattle and listened idly to the Bush voices talking round him. He heard far more than you would ever hear—voices of whispering leaves and boughs, of rustling grass, and softly-moving bodies. Not a grasshopper could brush through a tussock but Wurip knew that it had passed. Overhead, birds were twittering gaily in the branches. He knew them all—had he been hungry he might have wanted to set snares for some of the little chirping things, but just then he was too well-fed and lazy to trouble about such tiny morsels. He bit long grass-stems lazily, and tried to sleep.

A pair of jays flew into a tree close by, and began to chatter to each other, and suddenly Wurip found that he knew what they were saying. Somehow, it did not seem surprising that he should know. Afterwards he wondered if he had dreamed it, but at the moment nothing was strange to him. The jays, eager and chattering, did not notice the little black figure in the grass. They were too full of their subject.

"The Fire-Women have nearly finished their weaving," said one. "Soon the last mat will be done. They have worked very quickly since Wurip brought them rushes."

"And then they will go away," said the other.

"Yes, then they will go quite away, and there will be no more Fire for ever. He-he! what would the tribe say!"

"And Wurip!"

"Yes, Wurip also. What will he do when they have gone?"

"He will go back to his people, I suppose. He cannot go with the Fire-Women. I think, brother," said the smaller jay, "that they mean to sail away on their mats to another country, taking Fire with them."

"Certainly they mean to go, and to take Fire with them; did we not hear them talking about it while we perched on their wurley?" said the other. "As for sailing away on their mats, I do not see now that can be. Mats are not like wings. You are a foolish young bird."

"Well, why do they make them so strong and large, and how else will they get away?" asked the other, looking down his beak in an abashed way, but still sticking to his point. "You cannot tell me those things."

"I do not care to know," said the big jay; and that was untrue, because jays are very inquisitive. "What does it matter? They are only humans. But wonder what Wurip would say, if he knew."

"Wurip thinks he will take Fire back to the tribe. But I do not think he will ever get it. The Fire-Women watch him too closely—and anyhow, he is only a little cripple."

"He would be excited if he knew what we heard them say—that if they lost any of it now, all the rest would go out, and then their power would leave them, so that they could work no more Magic."

"He-he-he!" chattered the other jay. "But he will never know that. They do not talk when he is near."

"No, they are wise. It is a very foolish thing to talk," said his brother solemnly. Yet they chattered for a little while longer, and then they flew away.

Wurip lay motionless under the wattle-tree, and forgot to bite grass-stems anymore. He was not sure whether he was awake or dreaming; and he did not greatly care, because he felt that the warning that had come to him was true, whether he had dreamed it or not.

It fitted in with little things he had noticed. Lately the Fire-Women had been very busy at their weaving, working night and day, so that he could hardly bring them rushes quickly enough. A great pile of mats lay ready in a corner of their wurley, and now they were working together at the largest of all. They had seemed restless and excited, too, and talked earnestly together, although they were careful not to let him hear anything, and never to let him go near the fire. Not that they seemed to fear now that he would try to approach it. Wurip had been very careful, never even glancing towards it as he worked about the camp. He was allowed to place his firewood at a certain spot, and took great pains not to go beyond it. In every way in his power he used to try to make them think that he was afraid of Fire and dreaded to go too close to it since he had burned his arm. By this means he seemed to have put their suspicions to sleep, and they regarded him as a harmless little fellow, of whom they need have no fear.

He made his way back to the camp, slowly, thinking hard. If the Fire-Women were really going away, he must act, and act quickly. At anytime they might finish their work; and then they would disappear for ever, and there would be no more Fire to warm the people of the earth. Wurip drew up his thin little body as he walked, and clenched his fist. He made up his mind that he would act that very night.

He found the camp just as usual, with the Fire-Women working at their greatest mat of all, weaving it in and out in a curious device of green and white. One held the white strands, and the other the green; and their black hands worked so quickly that Wurip could scarcely see to which woman they belonged. He looked at it with great admiration, and ventured a timid word of praise. Then he went a little way off and began to skin the native cats and bandicoots that he had brought home.

When he had prepared them for cooking, he laid them carefully on crossed sticks and put them in a shady corner. It was growing dusk, and he hurried off to find firewood. All the time, he was turning many plans over and over in his mind, and rejecting one after another as useless. Well, he thought, he must trust to luck.

He came back to the camp with his bundle of wood, and began to heap it in the accustomed place, keeping a respectful distance from the Fire, and bending down his eyes, lest their burning desire should be seen. Already the sun had gone away over the edge of the world, and darkness was coming fast. The Fire-Women had been forced to stop weaving, for the pattern of the great mat was too fine to weave by firelight. Generally, when they had finished, one carried the work into the wurley while the other remained outside to watch Wurip and begin the cooking. But the great mat was now too heavy for one to lift, and so they rolled it up, and carried it away together.

Wurip, crouching over his heap of firewood, felt his body suddenly stiffened like a steel spring. Under his brows he watched them; and as the wurley hid them, he darted forward, snatched a big fire-stick from the glowing coals, and fled, with great noiseless bounds that carried him in a moment far into the dusk. Behind him he heard a sudden loud anguished cry, and knew that the Fire-Women had found out his theft.

For a moment he feared that the magic wall would spring up to bar his way, and he ran as he had never run before. But it did not come; and into his mind swept the words of the jay, that if Fire were taken from the Women, they would lose their power of Magic. He hardly dared to think that could be so—but as he ran on, finding no unseen obstacle in his way, hope surged over him. Magic was a thing against which no man could fight. But if he had only ordinary women to deal with, he was not afraid.

A few hundred yards from the wurley, he glanced back, and saw that their fire no longer sent its red gleam into the dusk. His heart leapt with joy, for it seemed as if the jays' story must be true; and if so, the Fire-Women's hearth was cold, and already the only Fire in the world was what he carried. The greatness of the thought caught his breath— surely such an honour should be for the bravest warrior of the tribe, and not for a half-crippled, undersized weakling like him. And behind him came a sudden trampling of running feet, and a cry of such terrible anger that the very waterfowl in the swamps hid themselves in fear. The Fire-Women were on his track.

Wurip ran forward, leaping from tussock to tussock sometimes slipping into bog-holes, and scratching his bare limbs on great clumps of sword-grass. In his withered hand he clutched the fire-stick; the other held his waddy, and sometimes he was glad to use it to help himself over rough places. Luckily, he knew the ground well—there was no part of it that he had not studied on his days out hunting, knowing that at anytime he might have to make his dash for home. He hid the glow of the fire-stick as much as he could, holding it so close to him that his skin was scorched by it; but his precautions could not conceal it altogether, and to the Fire-Women behind him it was like a red star, twinkling low down upon earth.

They came after Wurip swiftly. At first they had uttered savage cries of wrath, and fierce threats of what they would do to Wurip when they caught him; but soon it seemed that they knew that shouts and threats were useless, and after that they hunted him silently, only the quick pad of their feet being heard in the darkness. They were terribly quick feet. Wurip had not dreamed that women could run so fast. Sometimes, as the moon rose, he could see them in pursuit, grim and revengeful, looking like giants in the darkness. His soul was full of terror at the thought of what they would do if they caught him, for he knew that he would be but a little child in their hands.

They crossed the swamps and morasses, and the reed-fringed creeks—and here Wurip lost ground, for he had to go very carefully, lest he should slip and so drown the precious fire-stick that he held close to him. Only a blackfellow could have kept it alight so long; but Wurip knew just how to hold it so that the air fanned it enough to keep the dull coals glowing, without letting it burn too quickly away. He heard the Fire-Women splash through the creeks, not far behind him. Then they came into the scrub-country, all running at their wildest speed, for this was the last part of the journey back to the tribe.

Then Wurip knew that he must be beaten. He was nearly done— his breath came unevenly, and his limbs were like lead, and would no longer do his bidding. Fierce and untired, close behind him, came the Fire-Women. A little ahead, he knew of a bed of green bracken fern in a gully, and he set his teeth in the resolve to get thus far.

They were quite near him when the dark line of the gully showed, somewhat to his left. He threw all his remaining strength into a last spurt of energy, and then, turning from the straight line towards the camp of the tribe, he crept through the scrub to the gully, holding both hands over the fire so that it might not guide the Fire-Women to his place of refuge, and heedless of the cruel burning. He reached the gully safely, and flung himself face downwards among the rank ferns and nettles, panting as if his heart would burst from his body. He heard the Women run past, tirelessly swift; there came to him their angry voices, calling softly, lest they should miss each other in the dim scrub. They had not seen him swerve—that was clear; and Wurip hugged himself with joy to think that for the moment he was safe.

When they had passed, and the sound of their feet had died away, he crept from his gully and fled in a northerly direction. He ran all through the dark hours, with long trotting strides, as a dingo runs, and circling round so that he might miss the Fire-Women and come upon the camp from the other side. Sometimes he paused to rest, listening for the sound of the other hastening feet—but they did not come, and at last he believed that he had escaped pursuit.

He was very tired—so tired that at last he lost something of the blackfellow's keenness that guides him through even unknown country in the dark. Something seemed to have broken in his chest, from the time of his last mad spurt from the Fire-Women, and now each breath stabbed him. Perhaps it was because he was so tired that at last he became confused altogether, and swerved from the track he had mapped out for himself to get back to the camp; and when dawn broke he was back in the direction where he might expect to meet pursuit. Even as this dawned upon him, he looked up and saw the Fire-Women running silently towards him, their fierce eyes gleaming.

Wurip knew it was the end. He fled, knowing as he went that he could not run far. Behind him came the Women, tireless as though they had not spent the night in fruitless chase. He clutched the fire-stick to him, scarcely knowing that it burned his hands and his naked chest.

Rounding a clump of saplings, a sob burst from his labouring chest. Before him he saw the familiar camp, the wurleys clustered together; it seemed to smile at him in home-like fashion. So near home, to fail! He spurred himself to the last effort.

Then from the camp burst a knot of fighting-men, racing towards him. He caught the glint of the rising sun on their spears and throwing-sticks; and he waved to them, for he could not shout. They came on with great strides: there was music in the sound of their trampling feet. When they came to him, they divided, running past him, and Wurip staggered through the lane they formed. He heard fierce cries and blows behind him, but he did not stop.

Before him the camp lay, and never had it smiled to him a welcome so sweet. There were people running out to meet him; men, women, and little children: he could hear their voices, amazed and rejoicing— "Wurip! It is Wurip, bringing us Fire!" He tried to smile at them, but his lips would not move. So he staggered in to the circle of the huts, and there fell upon his face, still grasping the red fire-stick in his blistered hand. It was all red now, for it had burned down to the last few inches.

MARY GRANT BRUCE

Then, as they clustered round him, lifting him with gentle hands and blessing his name, he smiled at them a little, and died peacefully, happy that he had brought back Fire to his own people.

But to the people he did not die. Ever after they honoured his name, calling him the benefactor of the tribe: so that in death he found that honour that forgot he had ever been little and weak, and a cripple. And when you see the little Fire-tailed Finch that hops about so fearlessly, with the bright red feathers making a patch of flame on its sober plumage, you are looking at Wurip, the Fire-bringer, who gave his life to vanquish the wicked Fire-Women and to lay Fire once more upon the hearth-stones of his tribe.

A Note About the Author

Mary Grant Bruce (1878–1958) was an Australian journalist and children's book author. Born in Gippsland to Irish and Welsh Australians, Bruce attended Miss Estelle Beausire's Ladies High School before establishing herself as a leading journalist and poet. Her 1910 novel *A Little Bush Maid* launched the hugely successful *Billabong* series of bestselling children's novels. In 1913, she met her husband Major George Evans Bruce on a trip to London and returned with him to Australia, where they raised two sons. During the First World War, the family moved to Ireland while George served in Europe, inspiring her 1916 war novel *Jim and Wally*. Back in Australia, she continued to work on her *Billabong* series while publishing novels for adults and working as an editor for *Women's World* magazine. Towards the end of her life, having lost her husband and youngest son, Bruce settled in England, where she would remain until her death. Recognized as a pioneering writer whose works helped define Australian national identity, Bruce has been the subject of controversy for her racist portrayal of Aborigines and immigrants.

A Note from the Publisher

Spanning many genres, from non-fiction essays to literature classics to children's books and lyric poetry, Mint Edition books showcase the master works of our time in a modern new package. The text is freshly typeset, is clean and easy to read, and features a new note about the author in each volume. Many books also include exclusive new introductory material. Every book boasts a striking new cover, which makes it as appropriate for collecting as it is for gift giving. Mint Edition books are only printed when a reader orders them, so natural resources are not wasted. We're proud that our books are never manufactured in excess and exist only in the exact quantity they need to be read and enjoyed.

bookfinity™

Discover more of your favorite classics with Bookfinity™.

- Track your reading with custom book lists.
- Get great book recommendations for your personalized Reader Type.
- Add reviews for your favorite books.
- AND MUCH MORE!

Visit **bookfinity.com** and take the fun Reader Type quiz to get started.

Enjoy our classic and modern companion pairings!

Classic & Modern